"I will not slink about my house like a thief in the night, Elinor. I don't care if the whole world knows."

"Then we shall tell everyone I sat here for hours dishabille with you in the night."

Lucas smiled. "Your reputation will be forever ruined."

"Be that as it may, I'm not very worried. I'm not a society miss searching for an advantageous match." She stood, smoothing her dressing gown. Clearly, she looked a bit discomfited as she thought about their situation.

"Thank you for lending an ear to my strange tales. I think I can now bear the thought that I met a ghost tonight."

"More than one, I'd say. You met the ghosts of your past, whether you like it or not."

He stood and looked down at her earnest, open face. "You're right, but to what purpose?"

"You might discover a more compassionate side to your character."

"Compassion equals softness to me, an invitation to new hurts."

"Love does not hurt. Lack of love does."

He stared into her face for a long moment, longing deep in his heart . . .

BOOK YOUR PLACE ON OUR WEBSITE AND MAKE THE READING CONNECTION!

We've created a customized website just for our very special readers, where you can get the inside scoop on everything that's going on with Zebra, Pinnacle and Kensington books.

When you come online, you'll have the exciting opportunity to:

- View covers of upcoming books
- Read sample chapters
- Learn about our future publishing schedule (listed by publication month *and author*)
- Find out when your favorite authors will be visiting a city near you
- Search for and order backlist books from our online catalog
- Check out author bios and background information
- Send e-mail to your favorite authors
- Meet the Kensington staff online
- Join us in weekly chats with authors, readers and other guests
- Get writing guidelines
- AND MUCH MORE!

**Visit our website at
http://www.kensingtonbooks.com**

A CHRISTMAS BLESSING

Maria Greene

ZEBRA BOOKS
Kensington Publishing Corp.
http://www.kensingtonbooks.com

ZEBRA BOOKS are published by

Kensington Publishing Corp.
850 Third Avenue
New York, NY 10022

All Kensington titles, imprints and distributed lines are available at special quantity discounts for bulk purchases for sales
promotion, premiums, fund-raising, educational or institu-
tional use.

Special book excerpts or customized printings can also be created to fit specific needs. For details, write or phone the office
of the Kensington Special Sales Manager: Kensington Publishing Corp., 850 Third Avenue, New York, NY 10022. Attn.
Special Sales Department. Phone: 1-800-221-2647.

Zebra and the Z logo Reg. U.S. Pat. & TM Off.

First Printing: October 2002
10 9 8 7 6 5 4 3 2 1

Printed in the United States of America

For Pierre

One

The cold in the room clutched every cell of his body—it always would, Lucas Chandler, Earl of Lyons, thought as he looked into the blackness outside the window. The only light was one feeble lamp along the street.

The drizzle had turned into snow and the wind whined in the crack between window and frame. Great icy flakes tumbled outside, and he shivered. Delicate patterns of frost etched the glass, artwork only nature could create.

Not that he cared one iota about it; nothing changed the reality of his misery, no matter how beautiful.

He turned back to the room and watched his secretary, Ian Brinkley, bending over the accounts and painstakingly entering numbers with a goose quill. The fellow never complained about the cold in the mansion in Grosvenor Square, nor did he gripe about the mountain of work that awaited him every morning. In fact, he had an intolerably sunny disposition most of the time.

"My lord, this November is the coldest one in history, I believe," Brinkley said as he raised his eyes from the documents. "But the snow is always delightful. The children like it even if the temperatures are dropping steadily."

Lucas noted Ian's kind eyes behind the spectacles and the graying hair tied into an old-fashioned queue. He nodded. "Yes, we're in for an arctic winter. The fireplaces in this old heap can't keep up, no matter how high the fires are stoked."

Brinkley glanced at the fireplace, where logs smoldered and smoked. "The engineering wasn't done correctly, my lord, but it's a grand old place, proud and full of history." He scratched his head and hesitated as if debating whether to speak or not. "What it needs most is the cheerful sounds of people. 'Tis too quiet inside."

"Like a tomb, perhaps?" Lucas heaved a deep sigh. "I'm not looking for company. 'Tis the last thought on my mind."

"'Twould do you good, my lord, if you don't mind my saying so."

Lucas gave him a hard stare. "The woman is gone, and so are the parties and gatherings, Brinkley. I never was anything like her."

"Aye . . . but there's the little girl."

Lucas turned abruptly away. He didn't want to think about Annabelle, who had golden locks and cerulean blue eyes, so contrary to his own gypsy eyes and raven black hair. Annie's presence was a constant insult, a reminder of the parody of his marriage and the failure of his life.

He clenched his jaw and balled his hands into tight fists. The walls of steel that had started surrounding him after Phoebe's death were getting tighter, and sometimes he woke up in the middle of the night feeling as if he could not breathe. He felt guarded by a sentry of black thoughts which multiplied at night, tormenting him.

"Don't bring up Annie to me, Brinkley. I know you're concerned, but I'm not planning anything different for Christmas, or any other time. Yuletide just doesn't exist for me any more."

"But the little one needs to experience the joys of Christmas, my lord." Brinkley's forehead pleated with concern and his eyes darkened with distress. "She hasn't done anything wrong."

Lucas turned his gaze fully toward his long-time servant, his shoulders tight and pain shooting behind his eyelids. "I understand. I also accept you would take the liberty to speak up about it, but nothing has changed. I don't care that Christmas is only six weeks away."

Brinkley's head drooped as he turned back to the ledgers. "Very well, my lord. I was out of order to speak as I did."

Brinkley's words hung heavily in the air. They would hang there forever, no doubt, as a reminder of Lucas's burdened conscience. But he had tried to feel something for Annie, to no avail. The pain of it all was becoming too much to bear. He didn't know how much longer he could go on, and he certainly didn't have any desire to celebrate Christmas with her, or with anyone else.

He sat in the wing chair by the fire and poured himself a glass of claret from the bottle on the side table. Christmas truly meant nothing to him, nor did he understand the excitement over the decorations, the carol singing, and the lavish food, which invariably turned out to produce a stomachache.

Betrayal and disloyalty were his gifts from people who had professed to love him. Christmas two years ago had brought just such gifts, and those were hard to forget.

A knock sounded on the door and Winslow, the rotund and very proper butler, entered. Lucas sent him a cursory glance.

"My lord, your cousin, Mr. Nelson is here."

"The fool's out in this weather?" Lucas heard a commotion at the door and saw his cousin standing there, somewhat portly but fit, boots sprinkled with snow and flakes glittering in his hair.

Simon laughed and brushed at the snow that had strayed to his shirt cuffs. His face had the look of a cherub, one of those round, rosy ones that smiled perpetually in portraits in art galleries. Sometimes Lucas wondered if Simon ever had anything happen to him that brought him low. He doubted it. The man never had a bad day—at least not that Lucas could recall.

Simon was a cork that floated comfortably on the surface of the deep, dark sea of emotion, and if someone tried to push him down, he would bounce right back up. Sometimes Simon's stout good humor could be very wearying; he rarely offered a negative word or observation.

"Coz, you're sitting here alone in the gloom and

the cold. Where are all the candles and the merry fires? And the smells of good, plentiful food?"

"As you know, they don't exist here." Lucas motioned to the brocade-covered chair across from him and offered a glass of wine.

"Balderdash," Simon exclaimed. "I know your cupboards are filled with the best candles, and your larders overflowing. Mrs. Braithewaite wouldn't have it any other way, excellent housekeeper that she is. Not to mention Mrs. Miller, your excellent cook."

"Hmm."

"Oh what a glorious night! The snowflakes are a true wonder, so large but delicate, so lovely. This is the first real snowfall we've had this season. 'Tis always a thrill. I stood fifteen minutes just gazing at it falling."

"Nothing to be ecstatic about, surely. It's cold and the snow makes dirty slush on the streets eventually," Lucas replied gloomily.

"If only you changed your outlook a bit, dear fellow, you'd find life is not a burden, but a true joy. There's beauty everywhere you turn."

"So you keep telling me, Simon."

Simon sighed heavily, and the silence settled like a pall over the room. Brinkley's goose quill rasped over the pages, and within minutes he'd blotted the last entry and settled the books. It was late.

Lucas glanced up at his employee as Brinkley pushed his chair back and gathered his belongings. No doubt would he go home to a warm meal and the embrace of a kind wife.

"Good night, Brinkley."

"Good night, my lord." He donned cloak and hat and wound a long red scarf around his neck. Then he went across the room and stirred the logs in the fire. Instantly, warm orange flames leaped and bounced, bringing more cheer to the men sitting in front of it.

"See?" Simon commented. "All you had to do was to stir the fire for more warmth."

Brinkley left, closing the door softly behind him.

"The man is worth his weight in gold," Simon said. "A more loyal man you'll never find."

"Yes . . . that he is. Never a word of grievance from him, no matter how much work I give him."

Simon nodded. "You've been fortunate in your staff, Coz. Everyone is loyal and honest—which brings me to the reason I stopped by tonight."

"Oh, you *didn't* have an unquenchable desire to set my life straight?" Lucas chided. "I thought mayhap you braved the storm just to have a glass of claret with me."

"Your sarcasm has no impact on me," Simon said severely. "Plague take it, you have everything and still you complain as if your life has no meaning."

"It doesn't."

Tense silence hung for a moment, but Simon rallied, his good humor dimmed for only a second.

"The family has agreed something has to be done with Annabelle."

Lucas felt his chest tighten as Simon mentioned her name. "If you're coming as an emissary to ask that she be removed from my household, I must again make it clear that I take my responsibilities seriously. I'll never shirk my duty as a parent and fob her off on some relative."

"I know that, Lucas. I've come to put a proposal in front of you, one you might like, and one that will bring great benefits to Annabelle."

"I doubt it," Lucas replied, his mood falling even lower. "Well, just pummel me and then leave."

Simon didn't seem at the least daunted by those quelling words. "Annabelle is six. She'll need a governess soon, and I know the perfect woman for the job."

Lucas lifted his eyebrows.

"Elinor Browning is a distant relative to my father. She married Matthew Browning seven years ago, a younger son and an aide-de-camp to Wellington. The man unfortunately died at Salamanca, leaving the widow and her small son destitute. He didn't have much to call his own to start with, and this came as a doubly vicious blow emotionally and financially. Elinor has supported herself and her son with various positions, and she's well educated. In fact, she'll be the perfect governess to Annie. Her background is impeccable."

"Matthew Browning? His brother is Viscount Lyndhurst."

"The same. The gamester and wastrel. Whatever that family had in their coffers, Lyndhurst has run through."

"It must've been true and perfect love, since Matthew had no real prospects to offer a bride," Lucas said sarcastically.

"True love exists, you know," Simon said with a huff.

"Only in novels. As far as my observations among my cronies, not one has married for love. Matches have always been made for acquisition of property or a title—not to mention money."

"Mostly you're correct on that score, but there are exceptions."

Lucas snorted. "Only the blind and the naive believe that. There must've been something else with this paragon you mentioned and her husband. He probably got her in the family way and had to marry her."

"Dash it all, that's not true! They were married several years before little Alex arrived. He's four now."

Lucas had nothing to say to that.

"I've known her on and off as I grew up, but that side of the family, as you know, heralds from the north, not from the south counties like the Chandlers. Everyone said my mother married beneath herself when she married Arthur Nelson, but they are a good example of true love—in my opinion."

Lucas thought of his father's sister, so like Simon in looks. "I admit Nelson and Aunt Florence have gotten along famously, but that shouldn't make you so blind to reality. They *are* the exception."

Simon gave him a dark look. "'Tis hard for me to believe you are in any way related to my mother. She doesn't spend her life in gloom and doom."

Lucas nodded and gave a mirthless laugh. "Yes, 'tis a strange coincidence. Maybe I'm a foundling."

"You are agreeable to meet Elinor, then? I am doing you a favor, you know."

"I know you'll pester me until I agree, so, yes, I'll see this paragon."

"That's good, because I brought her with me tonight."

Lucas's jaw fell in surprise. "You did what?"

"No time like the present, Coz. I brought her with me, as she was very interested in the position when I mentioned it to her. She's been staying with us for a week and wants to find employment very badly."

"The poor relation, eh?"

"There's nothing poor about Elinor," Simon said stoutly.

Elinor sat on the uncomfortable carved settle in the foyer. As she waited, the gloomy air in the great mansion whittled away at her good humor. This wasn't exactly welcoming, she thought, even if the architecture of the building and the marble floors and exquisite furniture were attractive enough.

Only a few candles burned on the table by the door, and the fire in the fireplace had almost gone out. The lord of the manor must be a stingy sort.

She pulled her cloak more closely around her as she experienced second thoughts about the position. What was taking Simon so long? Was he struggling to convince the haughty earl of her brilliant qualities, or were they talking about the Pugilist Society and the latest bets at the clubs? You never knew with gentlemen. One thing was sure, she would not let anyone, no matter how toplofty, browbeat her into subservience.

She was always willing to work hard, but she'd never become a slave to anyone.

Her father might not have had a lofty title or even a "sir" tacked to his name, but he'd done his duty to king and country as a captain in the army and died at an old age with all of his medals of valor on the walls around him. That was more than could be said about most of the gentry.

She had been the apple of his eye, as she'd been born late, when her parents had lost all hope of having a child. No one had loved her as much as her father, not even her mother, though she'd also been loving and kind.

Elinor heard a commotion at the far end of the oblong foyer. Simon's tall form stepped out of the ornately carved door that must lead to the office, and he beckoned to her.

Elinor rose, her heart pounding with nervousness. If she couldn't accept this position, she would be in dire straits financially. She refused to sponge off her relatives any longer, even if they had been very supportive.

"Let's beard the wolf in his den," Simon whispered, and she felt another spurt of apprehension. "He's agreeable to see you."

Beard the wolf? Simon had told her Lord Lyons was a difficult sort due to past hurts, but she in all likelihood would have problems getting along with some dour predator. She pictured an older man with long graying hair, stooped shoulders, fangs at the ready, and a permanently sour expression on his face.

Startled, she discovered the opposite was true. The light from the fire leaped across Lord Lyons's face. She noticed the harsh planes, the strong jaw, and the beautiful deep brown eyes. He stood tall, his shoulders wide and proud, his bearing confident, definitely that of a lord. His dark hair waved away from a high forehead, and the flare of his eyebrows gave him an air of strength and determination. Why he would be so bitter, she could not understand.

He wore gray pantaloons that molded powerful legs, an immaculate coat of blue superfine, and the folds of his neckcloth lay with effortless elegance at his throat—every inch a man of fashion. But his expression was so remote, she thought.

Simon introduced them, and Lord Lyons bent over her hand and kissed the air right above her fingers. His movements were measured and sure, nothing extravagant, nothing revealing.

She lowered her eyes for a moment and made a curtsy, not too deep, not too shallow. As she extricated her hand from his grip, she looked into his eyes, which seemed full of shadows even as he looked right into her. Startled to feel her inner self revealed to him in a glance, she tore her gaze away and looked around the room.

The beauty of the tapestry on the wall, though wholly male in its depiction of a wild boar goring a deer to death, took her by surprise.

"What beautiful workmanship," she exclaimed and hurried across the chamber to take a better look.

"Flemish," the earl said, sounding bored. "It's ancient. We had it restored some years back."

She went on to admire other decorative items, among them two ornate bronze candelabra, other tapestries, and a frivolously patterned Chinese urn, in the rather stiff office. Simon had to clear his throat to bring her back to the business at hand.

"Elinor, Lord Lyons—"

"I would very much like to meet your daughter before I decide if I want the position or not," she said, plunging right in as she turned her gaze on the earl. "I'm sure Simon has explained my credentials, and that I'm eager for a position where I can help develop a young mind. However, I don't know if Simon mentioned I have a young son. He will have to live with me at my place of work."

She waited in silence as the words sank into him, and she could almost see every thought going through his mind. Strangely enough, she felt as if she'd known the earl for a long time, even if this was the first time she'd laid eyes on him. Fate made the strangest turns at times.

"You would school him at the same time, Mrs. Browning?"

"Alex is too young as yet, but yes, I intend to educate him." She raised her chin as if to affirm her plans. Her eyes challenged him to object, but he didn't. His gaze measured hers for a long time as if trying to read her intentions, and she returned his scrutiny frankly and without wavering.

"I work hard and I have a good hand with children. Your daughter will be trained in all the important things a lady should know, but I also have a wide background of other subjects mostly taught to young boys."

"Don't tell me you're a militant bluestocking, Mrs. Browning," he drawled, a cool smile hovering at the corners of his lips.

She shook her head. "I don't accept being labeled as affiliated with any kind of group. I believe in enlightened minds, be they male or female. It would be a pity not to develop bright talents."

"A liberal for sure," he muttered. "Well, I can't see any harm in that, as long as we're not nurturing future rebels under this roof."

She laughed out loud, and the sound echoed around the large room, somehow penetrating the gloom all the way to the corners.

Simon scratched his neck as if surprised at her animated outburst, but laughed in return. The earl didn't seem to notice. He only looked into the distance as if he'd lost interest.

Lucas *did* notice. He noticed it very much. No such sound had filled the house for as long as he could remember. It reminded him of the infectious gurgle of a silver brook on a sunny spring day, and it seemed to stay in the room even after she'd stopped laughing.

Had this always been such a tomb? Not that he cared much whether it was or not. He certainly couldn't change what had gone on with the generations before him within these walls, but was he slowly becoming like them?

He turned away briefly, trying to get his bearings. This had all come as such a surprise. Mrs. Browning's oval face held a vibrancy that was hard to ignore. Her hair, reddish with golden glints, curled in abandonment, even if she'd done her best to tame it into a chignon, and her frivolous hat perched atop all that glory with a saucy ostrich feather curling down to a straight, long neck.

She was tall, her bearing proud, her complexion creamy and flawless, and her eyes—*her eyes* a molten blue, he thought, due to the glint of light that pierced him every time he looked into them. Life positively bubbled out of her.

He wanted to say no, he wouldn't hire anyone just yet for Annabelle, but somehow he couldn't form the words.

He strode to the door and summoned the footman outside. "William, please fetch Lady Annabelle's nanny."

They stood in silence as they waited. Mrs. Browning flitted around the room, admiring the carved mahogany paneling and some ancient vases in a most unfitting manner, Lucas thought dourly. Was she of such mercurial temper that she couldn't stand still for even a moment? She might prove to be too energetic for his taste.

Miss Wendell, the nanny, appeared, curtsied, and stood timidly by the door.

"Miss Wendell, I know it's rather late, but please bring Lady Annabelle to me."

The young woman's eyes darted from one to the other as if understanding the situation. She curtsied again and left the room to obey his command. Another trickle of uncomfortable silence fell, and Simon started rocking on his feet.

When the knock came, Mrs. Browning and Simon turned expectantly toward the door, but Lucas turned away. He went, as always, to stare out the window, where only a few lights bobbed along as carriages passed on the street outside.

"Good evening, Annabelle," said Mrs. Browning in her melodious voice. He heard a rustle of skirts as she crossed the room to the child.

He glanced over his shoulder, and Annie curtsied as told by her nanny. The child stared at Mrs. Browning with distrust, then darted a glance at him. He hastily averted his eyes.

"Cousin Simon," Annie cried and ran to the one man who could coax full sentences out of her. She hugged his legs, and Simon hoisted her into his arms. Lucas's heart squeezed with pain as he watched from the corner of his eye.

"My sweet Annie! I have brought a wonderful surprise to you this evening. Mrs. Browning will be your new governess. I know you'll get along famously. She's a dear friend of mine, and she has a son named Alex. You'll have a little playmate."

Lucas turned to witness the exchange fully. To

her credit, Mrs. Browning joined Simon and took Annie's hand. "I promise we'll be friends, and I'll teach you how to read and write. That will open up a whole new world for you."

Annie obviously couldn't grasp the concept, but she stared at Mrs. Browning with large, searching eyes. "Sometimes Simon reads me a story. I like that."

"You will hear many, many stories, and you'll make up some of your own. You have such beautiful golden curls!" Mrs. Browning continued, touching one bouncing ringlet. "And such blue eyes."

Lucas closed his eyes and swallowed the bile rising in his throat. He shouldn't have drunk that much claret.

He heard Mrs. Browning chattering away with Annie, and the girl responded in monosyllables. It would take time to forge a connection, because Annie spent a lot of her time in isolation with Miss Wendell in the nursery.

Mrs. Browning's infectious laughter echoed more than once in the room, and Lucas fought the suggestion of relaxation and pleasure that it offered.

For a moment he felt as if his world was coming apart. Then he struggled to bring the walls of protection back up around him.

When Miss Wendell had taken the girl back upstairs, he joined Simon and Mrs. Browning by the fireplace. They were both warming themselves by the smoking logs, and Lucas stirred the fire with a poker to extract more life from the flames. He had little success.

"I would like to accept the position," Mrs. Browning said. "Your little daughter is adorable, and I'm sure we'll get along famously."

Lucas nodded, wondering if he really wanted another servant in the house, one who might eat at his table. He had no desire for lectures and animated discussions about the latest books and fashions.

"I would like to suggest a trial period of two months to see how well you fit into Annie's life and the household at large."

Mrs. Browning accepted that with a nod of her head. She had a decidedly stubborn set to her chin, he thought, which might bode ill. But on the other hand, Mrs. Browning evidently was of the independent sort, so she would stay out of his way. That was the only way he could tolerate living with her under the same roof.

"I expect you to solve problems as they arise without running to me every time," he said, to affirm his earlier thought.

"I'm skilled at that, as I have a child of my own. Do you need to meet Alex before we settle everything?"

"No, there's absolutely no need. I won't be having anything to do with him."

Her mouth pinched into a thin, hard line, and her eyes held a fleeting expression of—pity? He wasn't sure. But why would she pity him?

"I'll have my servants sent over to pick up your belongings," he said dismissively.

"Coz, that's not necessary," Simon said. "My people will deliver her things."

Lucas looked at Mrs. Browning, noting again her proud bearing. She might prove too difficult, but he'd take a chance. At least he knew whence she heralded, and he trusted Simon implicitly. Simon would not fob some impossible female on him. He knew better.

"My butler will show you around your quarters and the schoolroom. When you've settled in, we shall go over your curriculum."

"That sounds acceptable to me," she said, too haughtily in his opinion.

With a stiff bow, he dismissed them both, but he could've sworn a smile lurked at the corners of her mouth.

There really was nothing to smile about.

TWO

Elinor turned around as snow whirled about her and stared up at the tall, almost menacing building behind her. "I don't know how it'll be to live here," she said thoughtfully to Simon. "There's such a feeling of gloom over the whole house, and the lord is as frozen as the icicles hanging from the eaves."

"Your observation is very keen, Elinor," Simon said. "Lucas wasn't always this way. He was quite happy until he married. Things went wrong from the start. Then his wife died, and he's never been right since. 'Tis as if he's frozen in anger and despair."

"And he totally ignored his little girl. She ran to you, not to her father."

Simon shuffled his feet. "Lucas never had a good hand with children, I'm afraid. It was this way from the very beginning. He had no interest in Annie at all, but she knows he's her father and tried to form a bond, but gave up when he didn't respond."

"The man is emotionally crippled," she said firmly. "I shan't take any set downs from him, and if he has no communication with his daughter, I won't allow him to dictate my work. I will know better what she needs." She looked at Simon, who wore a worried expression. "Come now, Simon, you know me. I get my way with an abundance of charm, not harsh words."

Simon chuckled. "You're right on that score. Anyhow, you'll be very good with Annie, and I'm happy to do that small favor for the girl. She's much too lonesome as it is. You're just the right person to bring her up."

"I shall do my best. I promise you that."

Lucas stayed up for a long time that night. The house seemed haunted with old memories. He kept thinking about his own father, who had died alone upstairs after having made an enemy of anyone who cared for him. The very walls seemed steeped in his bitterness.

Lucas heaved a profound sigh and rose from his chair by the fireplace. He should be tired by now after all the claret he'd drunk, but he felt only strangely disoriented. Seeing Annie had made his heart heavy. Guilt ate at him every waking hour, but he was unable to bridge the emotional gap between them. Physically, Annie had everything, but not his love.

He went upstairs, noting a slight dizziness from the wine. In his bedroom, he dismissed Morris, his valet, and undressed himself. All he ever wanted was to be alone and at peace. He didn't need females laughing in his house or children running amok.

When Mrs. Browning moved in, he would make sure she stayed totally out of his way. She could take her dinners on a tray.

He sat on the edge of the mattress. The old green-and-gold velvet bed hangings seemed to close in on him tonight, and he still felt some dizziness and a hint of nausea. Maybe he'd eaten something that didn't agree with him. The turbot could've been slightly off.

He leaned his head into his hands and felt the weight of his despondency. As he sat there, the dizziness increased, making his head spin uncontrollably. He lay down, his forearm covering his eyes.

An icy draft crept across the room, and he wondered if Morris had forgotten to close the windows. Why they would be open at all was a mystery to him. The draft increased, and he swore under his breath. He would have to get up.

He opened his eyes and struggled to sit up. The room was bathed in an eerie glow, a milky green mist that seemed illuminated from inside. He rubbed his eyes and stared again. *Still there,* he thought, perturbed as he realized the cold was emanating from that strange glow.

His heart started pounding as the mist moved, coming closer to the bed. Dressed only in his shirt, Lucas shivered, but cold sweat formed on his forehead. The turbot must've been very bad to create such hallucinations. Unable to move, he stared at the mist that kept coming closer.

Fear gripped him as he noticed the middle of the mist had a human form. A ghost! He'd never seen one, but he'd heard people declare the mansion was haunted.

"Who are you?" he asked, his voice unsteady. He knew full well the specter wouldn't speak to him. Ghosts didn't talk—or did they?

He stared, unable to pull his gaze away. A vicious headache pounded at his temples, and he rubbed the area as he desperately tried to make some sense out of the apparition. Fear paralyzed him.

The ghost didn't move. It had glided so close he could almost touch it. He knew if he reached out, there would be nothing tangible there.

"I am your father," a faint but unmistakably familiar voice said. It had an inflection of heaviness, as if carrying too many burdens. He noticed the ghost dragged a ball and chain behind him as he moved even closer.

"Father?" Lucas croaked. "You're not like yourself. You never seemed so burdened in life."

The specter stared at him. Lucas could see a faint fire in the holes where there should be eyes. "Why are you here?" he forced out.

"I'm here to warn you."

"Warn me? How?"

"If you don't change your ways and keep placing emotional guilt and encumbrances on those who love you, you'll be cursed to wander the wastelands of the spirit world, dragging a ball and chain that grows heavier with every negative thought and deed you perform."

The voice was unquestionably that of the previous Lord Lyons, and Lucas felt a strong urge to cry. Emotions that had been trapped inside him for so long sought to push out, to burst a steel dam he didn't even know he had built. With enormous force, he pushed down the unpleasant feelings, but the weight didn't lessen. In fact, it had increased.

"'Tis wholly selfish to concentrate only on yourself and what you perceive as an injustice done to you," the transparent image of his father said.

The ghost seemed to want to impress the importance of his words. He enveloped Lucas in a cold more intense than anything he'd ever felt before.

"Lucas, this is where I am, in the frozen netherworlds. Sons tend to travel in their father's footsteps, but in this instance it would be the height of folly to go where I have led. I was the coldest, most selfish man alive, and I regret my actions as I suffer now."

"I don't recall that you were that much of an ogre, Father. Then again I didn't see much of you."

"That is part of my guilt. I treated you as if you were unimportant and a nuisance when I should've rejoiced in the blessing you were."

"My life is not like yours was, Father."

"It's slowly becoming just like that, an emotional wasteland. Little Annie deserves a loving father. She has no mother. She has only you and the servants, and they treat her better than you ever could. I'm deeply, unequivocally disappointed in you."

Lucas felt a stir of resentment. How could he be blamed under the circumstances?

"Self-pity is corroding you, and you don't even see it. Well, I am here to warn you, Lucas—a small payment on my own enormous debt."

Lucas shook his head, unable to believe this was happening. His dizziness had not abated, and he suspected if it did, he wouldn't be able to see the ghost.

"I'm not a figment of your imagination," the apparition said, as if it could read Lucas's thoughts.

"Nevertheless, you're made of thin air, not substance."

"In this dimension I'm as solid as a wall, Lucas, and ten times wiser than I was while walking on the earth. We're fools when living in our fortresses of fear and ignorance."

"I'm not afraid!" Lucas protested, even as apprehension clutched his middle.

"Your very denial speaks of ill-advised stubbornness. Ultimately, you'll lose everything if you cling to your belief that you have to close everyone out of your life. You need to examine your thoughts on this." The ghost started fading. "The remedy to all ills is to live with an open heart," he added, his voice growing fainter with every word.

Lucas reached out, trying to hold back the mist. "Don't leave me now. You've only just started talking to me, and in a way you never talked to me before."

"I have no peace; I travel the ethers constantly. As part of my atonement, I speak to people like you. It makes this ball and chain lighter." He pointed to the iron ball, which looked very insubstantial, in Lucas's opinion.

"My ball also grows heavier every time a soul I hurt in any way passes over. I have to accept the constant burden of that. Lucas, if you don't mend your ways, you'll be haunted by apparitions created from your own fears. They shall visit you in the night."

Lucas stared at the specter, trying to decide whether this was really happening. It had to be. The words were real enough. They positively hung in the room even as the milky glow dimmed and Lucas found himself alone.

He stood on shaky legs and walked to the spot where the ghost had been standing. A remaining chill was the only suggestion this vision had taken place at all. He shook his head, stepped across the room, and pulled the heavy green velvet drapes aside. Opening the window, he dragged cold air deeply into his lungs to clear his confusion.

The Watch, walking on the street below with his lamp on a stick, called out, "Twelve o'clock and everything is calm."

How could he say such a thing when specters were afoot and threats of eternal condemnation hung in the air?

Lucas shut the window abruptly and pulled the drapes closed. He went back to his bed, his legs now as heavy as if truly weighted with lead balls. With a sigh, he sank down onto the soft mattress.

He knew sleep would elude him tonight. His

thoughts kept circling around what the ghost of his father had said. He highly doubted the accusations applied to himself, but a nagging feeling at the edges of his mind wouldn't go away.

It had startled and pained him beyond measure to see his father suffer even after he'd left this mortal plain. He had suffered much in life, mostly due to his stubborn and prideful disposition. Still, Lucas had never wished such a fate to befall his father, and there was nothing he could do about it.

Elinor sat in her bed, propped against pillows, and stared at the dancing flame of the candle on the bedstand. The kindness of the Nelsons had warmed her these last weeks, but she knew she couldn't live on their mercy for much longer. She had to fend for herself, and no opportunity had appeared except the governess post with Lord Lyons.

She felt an enormous reluctance to take the position, knowing that living in that gloomy mansion would put a damper on her usually high spirits. And God only knew how difficult it would be to rear the little girl. Annie had seemed amiable enough, but she carried scars of loneliness and rejection.

Elinor's heart went out to her. It would take time to bring out the sparkle in Annie's eyes.

Heaving a sigh, Elinor thought about the cold and remote earl. The Ice King, she called him in her mind, so handsome and so wholly inaccessible. Ice surely flowed in his veins, and it wasn't the cold steel of courage. It was the frozen fear of protection. Woe to he—or she—who would try to chip away at that. Not that she had the slightest desire to do so, but it irked her that someone so obviously blessed with health, wealth, and the loyalty of the people around him could be so obviously despondent. It was irresponsible, in her opinion.

If he had to struggle to eat, maybe he wouldn't be so self-absorbed, she mused. *He would have greater things to think about.*

The snow had turned to sleet outside. Pellets struck the windows with force, bony fingers knocking on the panes. She didn't know where she got that ghoulish image, and she was utterly grateful for her warm bed and the fire sparking merrily in the fireplace. Some people had to sleep outside, and as she thought of them, she sent out a prayer of mercy. Without her kind relatives, she and Alex could easily be part of that group of destitute people.

Her heart filled with gratitude and joy over the fact she had so much support in her life. She knew better than to worry about the future, she was strong, and she wouldn't let some Ice King dampen her spirits.

Three

Alex was running as fast as his chubby legs could handle. He loved the shiny hard floor in their new home, and he loved to slide over it in his stocking feet. He'd never seen a floor that vast. The house was more of a castle, something a king might live in. Mama would be upset if she found him here. She'd told him to stay in the servants' regions or the schoolroom, but he liked to explore.

He enjoyed himself so much he didn't notice the obstacle in his way. He careened straight into it, a hard pair of long legs that knocked the wind out of him.

Falling on his bottom, he glanced up at the tall man in front of him. His heart started to pound with fear. The man looked so forbidding. Maybe he *was* the king. *Maybe I'll get sent to my room for a week.*

"You ruined my run—the best one ever," Alex said cockily, wondering what kind of horrid punishment would be meted out after this. "I almost touched the door at the other side this time."

"You did? I'm surprised you're here at all. The foyer is not a playground for children. I have priceless vases from China in here, and if you broke one of those—"

"But I didn't, sir. I'm ever so careful, and please don't tell Mama."

"She wouldn't approve?" the tall man asked, smiling coldly.

"She would be ever so vexed if she found me here, but she thinks I'm having my tea with the servants."

"And you aren't."

"Aw, they eat that slow. I was done long before everyone else, so I came here to practice my run."

"I see." The man didn't look any kinder.

Alex smelled trouble. The foyer felt very cool all of a sudden.

"You've been at it before, I take it."

"I won't do it again, sir."

"I doubt very much you will."

"Are you the king, sir?"

That drew a reluctant laugh from the man. "No, most certainly not. The king is closeted at Windsor due to a mental illness. And I'm not the Prince Regent either."

"Oh." Alex felt relieved.

"You must be Alex Browning. You have your mother's red hair."

Alex hadn't thought of that. Would his mother have taken hair from her head and glued it to his?

"I don't, sir. If it were glued on, it wouldn't hurt when she pulls it."

"You're right, I suppose. Does she pull it a lot?"

"Only when I have been very bad."

"As you have today."

Alex pondered those words. "Mayhap, but Mama doesn't usually pull my hair. She talks an awful lot in a loud voice when she's vexed."

"And then you go and repeat exactly the same game, don't you? I bet you're just as stubborn as she is."

"You know my mama?"

"I'm Lord Lyons, her employer."

"Oh." A streak of fear went through Alex. What if Mama would lose her employment because of him? Alex stood and faced the man, his hands on his hips. "If you take away Mama's work, I shall call you out, sir."

Lord Lyons lifted his eyebrows and seemed to ponder the threat. His dark cloak looked frightening, like black wings, and he slapped the gloves in his hand against his thigh. "Would that be with pistols or with swords—sir?"

Alex thought for a moment and remembered the toy sword Uncle Simon had given him. "Swords, sir."

"At dawn? But that's very early for a young man like you."

"For Mama I'll do anything," Alex said stoutly.

"That is commendable," the man said with a sigh. Alex thought he looked very sad. "For that I won't dismiss your mother. Besides, she's been at her post for only a week."

"Will you . . . um, tell her about this?" Alex shuffled his feet on the floor. One stocking had slid forward to puddle at the tips of his toes, and he pulled it up guiltily.

"I . . . well, I will have to think about it," Lord Lyons said.

Rapid footsteps sounded on the stairs that circled the mighty walls where the old men in the paintings stared down.

"Alex! I've been looking everywhere for you! How dare you disobey my orders?"

Mama looked very vexed, her face red, her hair standing out in wild curls around her eyes as it always did when she was agitated.

"I'm sorry, Mama."

Elinor stared from the man to the boy and gripped Alex's arm. "You come with me this instant. I told you you're forbidden to play in the areas where Lord Lyons lives. How could you be so willful?"

"The boy surely meant no harm, Mrs. Browning."

"Mama, the floor is ever so slippery. Like ice. I slide like the wind."

Elinor heard the eagerness in Alex's voice and couldn't be angry with him for being a child wanting to explore. But his willfulness had to be curbed, or she would surely get a taste of Lord Lyons's displeasure.

"I shall talk to you later, Alex. For now, run upstairs and stay in your room. You shall have no supper."

Alex gathered his shoes and fled up the stairs. Elinor stood uncertain in front of her employer. He didn't look angry, just drawn.

"I apologize for his behavior, my lord."

"He's four, you said?"

She nodded. An odd sort of tension hung between them. She couldn't quite put her finger on it, but it made her breathless and her heart pounded faster. Probably fear, she thought.

"He speaks very well for a four year old."

"Yes, he has always had a thirst for knowledge and started talking early. He's driven by his curiosity."

"Boys tend to be at that age," he said noncommittally, and she sensed he would let all of this pass without a reprimand.

"My lord, I'm happy to report Lady Annabelle is responding well to me. She's very withdrawn, but she's curious as well. She needs to be drawn out, and I feel Alex will be of great help. I surmise she hasn't had much contact with other children."

"You surmise correctly. I'll leave all of that to you, Mrs. Browning." He looked as if he wanted to change the subject as he flung his gloves on the nearest table.

"Surely you take great interest in your daughter's rearing?" Elinor was appalled to notice the apparent lack of concern in his demeanor, and she wanted to shake him. Damned Ice King!

"I haven't so far, and I doubt it'll change." He sounded infinitely weary.

Elinor didn't quite know what to say. She sensed many hidden layers of emotion trapped inside him, but she also felt angry at his obvious indifference. "Your statement is highly arrogant, in my opinion," she said, knowing full well she could lose her employment with such a statement. "This is about a child's life, a girl who needs all the support she can get to grow up strong and healthy."

He stared at her coldly with those deep, dark eyes, not saying a word, and at that moment she despised him.

"Is it because she's a girl, and not a boy?" Elinor couldn't believe her own gall, but the man behaved like a complete muttonhead.

A cool smile lurked at the corners of his beautiful mouth. "I was sure you were a bluestocking, and now I have proof. No such question would come from a traditional female."

"You're evading my question, and by that I presume I'm right."

"Don't jump to conclusions because I'm reluctant to take blame for your accusations."

"My lord, I believe everyone should be educated, not just the male species. Ladies were born with brains, too."

"Very superior brains," he drawled, and she felt heat rise in her cheeks. The gall of him! She took some deep breaths so as not to quarrel outright with him. She wouldn't want to give him that pleasure.

They stared at each other, and she read the silent challenge in his eyes. He drew the cloak of authority around him, a trait bred in him since his first breath. But how little it served him when it came to being truly human, she thought.

"I understand about bringing the lineage of the

family forward through sons," she began, "but I also have the opposite perspective that we must not forget: All lords had mothers. I try to look at things from every side."

"Are you implying I don't?"

She paused. "Possibly."

"You don't know me well enough to pass such a judgment."

"I see what is going on here at the mansion. Your home is gloomy and cheerless, the servants subdued, your child emotionally neglected."

Anger flared in his eyes. "She gets everything she needs."

"Everything that sustains her body, perhaps, but what about love and support?"

"I believe you've gone too far, Mrs. Browning." His face had darkened with anger, and his tone turned icy. "I will let this pass. We'll pretend we didn't have this conversation, but in the future, keep your tongue in order. Do not speak to me like this. I want only sporadic reports on Annabelle's progress, nothing more."

Red-hot anger gripped Elinor, but she would have to hold her tongue or find herself and Alex out on the street this very afternoon. She couldn't face going back to her relatives and asking for their assistance.

"Very well. I regret that I spoke out of turn, but my main concern lies with Annabelle. She's exceptionally bright."

"I'm glad to hear it." Without another word, he turned on his heel and left the foyer. She noticed his hair at the nape of his neck was still wet from the snow, and it curled beguilingly, giving him an air of innocence he definitely didn't have.

She felt a huge wave of frustration—and powerlessness to penetrate his armor. Besides, he would never be able to see her point of view. Why did she even try?

Just because the little girl deserved better. It had taken only one day in her company to know that and to fully understand the depth of her isolation.

She realized she wouldn't be able to let this treatment go on for any length of time. Lord Lyons would have to understand. She might lose her position in the process, but then so be it.

Lucas went into the library, the warmest room in the house. He felt restless and agitated. Mrs. Browning's words had nicked him like knife points. The nerve of her. She'd been in the house only a few days, and already she was putting demands on him in a tyrannical voice.

Winslow had already reported that the servants liked the new governess. She was friendly and humble, treating everyone as equals, not putting herself above the others, as was the custom with governesses. *Humble? Hardly*, he thought, swearing under his breath.

"She has a head full of common sense," Winslow had said, "and an abundance of charm. I haven't heard so much laughter in the kitchen since . . ." Winslow had let his words peter out, but Lucas had been acutely aware of the meaning. Since the days of the irresponsible Phoebe, the liveliest of butter-flies, the most heartless of creatures. But yes, Phoebe had had charm in abundance.

Lucas didn't trust charm.

He sat down at his desk to go over the accounts of Lyons Court, his country seat, but his mind kept wandering to Mrs. Browning's animated face. When she grew angry, her eyes sparkled with fire, and her cheeks flushed red. He didn't want to re-member the conversation. Just like the ghost of his father, she had touched a chord within him.

He must've dreamed that his father had ap-peared in the night. Yet the specter had been so real, so utterly convincing he couldn't dismiss the whole thing as a hallucination. It gave him chills to think about it. His father's warning had no bear-ing on the truth. Surely it was nobody's business how he chose to live his life.

Everyone was harping on him and pointing out his flaws, he thought sourly. Even the servants were giving him pitying glances. All he tried to do was to stay out of everyone's way, so why would they get in-volved in his problems and make a point of drawing him out?

He shut the ledgers with a slam. All he wanted was peace from everyone's prying eyes. He needed more time to forget the past, and no one needed to tell him how to do it and when to do it, *damn it all!*

A sudden knock on the door startled him out of his reverie. Winslow entered, carrying a tray with a bottle of claret and a glass. He set it down on the table by the fire, where Lucas enjoyed sipping a glass of wine and staring into the flames.

"Thank you, Winslow," he said. He rose, and as he did so he noticed a flash near the door—bright blue fabric and red tresses. Mrs. Browning. There was no mistaking that red hair anywhere. What did she want now?

She stepped inside, her cheeks red with embarrassment, her eyes sparkling with something—maybe battle? She waited until Winslow had left before she spoke.

"I'm sorry to intrude unannounced, but Annie was crying this afternoon, saying she missed her papa. I brought her down here for a few minutes, hoping you would take some time to speak with her. Console her, rather," she added.

Annie had been hiding behind Mrs. Browning's skirts and peeked at him from the folds. She looked frightened and worried, her lips drooping. For one wild second he wanted to say something to make her feel better, but nothing could induce him to move from the spot to which he'd frozen.

"Say good afternoon to your father, Annie," Mrs. Browning said brightly, and he cursed her under his breath.

"Actually—" he began.

"Good afternoon, Father," Annie said in a voice that wasn't much more than a whisper. Her eyes looked huge and dark in that round pale face. Freckles sprinkled her nose liberally, and her chubby hands clutched hard at the fabric of Mrs. Browning's gown.

"Hmmm . . . good afternoon," he replied awkwardly, all the time swearing silently at the governess's audacity—or maybe at his own inadequacy at handling the situation. Surely there was no need for this kind of confrontation.

"There, Annie, see?" Mrs. Browning said kindly. "He's still with us, and I suspect he's rather busy with his work." She turned to him. "You have to understand that Annie thought you'd moved away since you hired me to take care of her. When children get an idea into their heads—"

"There's no need to explain," he said tersely. "You're in sole charge with Miss Wendell. I trust you're more than capable of handling—"

"'Tis not a matter of *handling* as you put it, Lord Lyons," she said, her eyes flashing with anger. "Chil—people are not objects to be handled."

His chest felt tight with anger. "You are overstepping—"

"My boundaries. Lord Lyons, I know I'm a hired employee, but I'm also human, and when I see a need, or a lack that is in my power to fulfill, I act. There's no doubt in my mind that I'm doing the right thing, even if it means putting myself in danger of losing my post." She glanced at Annie, who looked at her with round eyes. Taking the girl's hand firmly in hers, she stared defiantly at Lucas.

He knew she expected him to send her packing. Wanting desperately to lash out, he hesitated. If anything, he had to admire her for her courage and her honesty. She wanted the best for Annie. He recognized the qualities because he'd had them himself once. He didn't now.

"Papa," Annie piped. "Mrs. Browning made me a doll." She held out one hand clamped rigidly around a cloth doll with a red dress and yellow yarn hair. He could see she'd painted a face painstakingly that displayed a happy smile. It was agony to look at Annie clutching that doll.

He turned to the woman he knew might cause his world to crumble—if he let her. "You can see I am busy, Mrs. Browning. 'Tis all well and good that you brought Annie downstairs, but now I have to get back to work."

A veil of something descended over her eyes for a moment. Then the molten flash was back. She didn't look happy at all. She should, he thought. After all, he hadn't dismissed her on the spot.

"You make *my* work very difficult, Lord Lyons," she said. She glanced at the girl, and he realized she was searching for words Annie wouldn't understand. "I work with the emotions of . . . living things, and you work with numbers. I feel a great responsibility to bring out the best in the next generation, and it's unfathomable to me that you can be so indifferent to that universal duty, let alone anything closer to home."

Resentment boiled in his stomach. "You can set yourself up as a judge over others, but you don't know the whole truth, so your judgment will be inaccurate."

She turned around, her blue skirt swishing against a table. Without another word, she pulled the child out of the room. Annie looked over her shoulder at him, her big blue eyes questioning him. He saw longing mix with disappointment. Then came resignation as her little shoulders drooped.

"Why is Papa vexed, Mrs. Browning?" she asked as they went through the doorway.

He could almost hear Mrs. Browning's unspoken words, *your father is an idiot,* but she said, "Your father is a very busy man, and we'll have to come back when he has more time to spend with you."

"When?" the child asked, her voice growing fainter as they moved down the hallway.

"Soon, Annie. Soon."

He wanted to yell after her not to put ideas into Annie's head, but he couldn't muster the energy.

For some reason he felt shame, but why should he? It was none of Mrs. Browning's business what he did with his life, or how he treated other people. He'd never said a harsh word to Annie, nor lifted a hand in anger, something he would point out if the dratted woman confronted him again.

Brushing aside the uncomfortable thoughts, he went back to the ledgers. Not that he really needed to go over the ledgers. Brinkley never made any mistakes.

Every one of his servants was efficient when dealing with his affairs, which reduced his work to very little. Perhaps it was about time he found something worthwhile to sink his energy into.

Four

Elinor could not believe the depth of Lord Lyons's callousness. How could he so completely ignore his daughter? Annie was the sweetest, most pliable child, not causing one moment of conflict. The little girl moved through life with grace and patience, and the only big cloud on her sky was her troubled relationship with the earl.

Elinor paced her room. She stopped and touched the mementoes she'd placed on the escritoire by the window. There was a small porcelain doll her father had given her when she turned ten, and the beautiful India shawl her husband had given her on their first anniversary. She touched the painted miniature of Matthew and felt that familiar longing. It had lessened considerably over the years since he passed, but in some corner of her heart she would always cherish him. He had been her first love, the one who had brought her from girlhood to womanhood. Their time together had been limited, but she'd seen enough of him for their love to deepen, and she had appreciated all the varied facets of marital life.

She blushed at the thought of missing the physical side of her marriage, but she did.

Standing face to face with the virile Lord Lyons had brought such thoughts back into her life, but any healthy man might inspire that part of her. Under no circumstances would she want to be involved with someone as flawed as Lord Lyons. What she needed was warmth and companionship, not someone frozen in an emotional ice block.

Not that she had any interest in his lordship, but she couldn't ignore her own longings for a special gentleman in her life.

She could take care of herself, but what she yearned to explore were the depths of feeling and intimacy that were possible in a marriage. Hers had been ruthlessly cut short before she and Matthew had had the chance to develop the depths she longed for.

She touched the silver-backed brush her mother had given her, and there were the old letters from her cousins—words of support always, but also lamentations that they could not afford another mouth to feed. That's when she'd gone out to earn a living.

Thank God her father had seen the importance of a well-rounded education for her. Her mother had been an expert in all the domestic skills and had possessed a talent for organization that Elinor had inherited.

"I do miss the things we used to do, the theater and the dances. Now I'm confined to the dreary upstairs life of a servant," she said out loud. "Neither fish nor fowl." Governesses held a in-between position few envied. She'd made a point to mix with all the strata of servants at the great house, from Winslow at the top, who liked her and she him, to the scullery maids and boot boy at the bottom.

"Oh, Matthew, I chafe against this confined life," she whispered. "But Annie and Alex need me." She had already come to love the little girl, and her son got along well with everyone, even the finicky Mrs. Braithewaite, the housekeeper. The scamp had found a special ally in Mrs. Miller, the head cook, who always stuck sweetmeats into his eager little hand.

She stood in front of the fire in the small fireplace and wondered what she could do to bring the earl and Annie closer together. The earl certainly was a nincompoop, but she also felt pity for the fact that he seemed unable to love anyone, including himself. The shards of pain were evident in his eyes.

Not that she could do anything about it—or could she? It might be a gamble, but her goal was to unite Annie with her father, and to do that the earl had to change his perception and his behavior. First his rigid world had to be demolished. She doubted she would be capable of playing the role of destroyer, but it was worth a try.

The next few days she endeavored to think of ways to make him take notice and change, but he wholly avoided her and the children. An optimist, though, she hoped an opportunity would present itself.

One morning she came across Mrs. Braithewaite in the upstairs hallway that led to the servants' quarters. She was arranging candles of different lengths and shapes. "I ordered some new candles for Christmas, Mrs. Browning, but I don't know how his lordship will allow for the cheer they might create," she lamented.

Elinor glanced into the round face and trusting blue eyes of the old housekeeper. A starched white cap perched on the severe gray knot on the top of her head, and her homespun roundgown was clean and pressed.

"I'd say you might as well fill all the candelabra, Mrs. Braithewaite. I'd wager his lordship won't notice. This mansion needs some comfort. We haven't seen the sun in weeks now."

"Aye. In the old days, her ladyship, the earl's mother, used to burn an abundance of candles, but after she died, no one took any interest in the house except for me," the housekeeper said with a sniff.

"It must've been an uphill battle for you." Elinor laid a comforting hand on the older woman's arm.

"Aye. We had a time when Phoebe, his lordship's wife, lived here, but her stay was rather short. She had flowers on all the tables and candles in every lowly candlestick. She passed on to her just rewards, alas."

"I don't see why you can't mimic what those ladies accomplished," Elinor said.

"The house itself seems to resent gaiety and laughter," the housekeeper muttered. She gave Elinor a calculating glance. "You, however, might have the strength to change it for yuletide. Would you help me decorate the halls?"

"Certainly," Elinor said with conviction. "All his lordship can do is to order us to remove the candles. But, as I said, I doubt he'll notice."

The housekeeper filled a basket with tapers and handed it to Elinor. "Would you mind taking care of the downstairs rooms?"

"Not at all." Elinor felt a spurt of excitement at the thought of Christmas. It was a time for cheer and closeness with those for whom one cared the most.

She took the heavy basket and walked down the curving grand staircase. Many ladies had walked down these steps dressed in their finest ball gowns, she thought, perhaps adoring husbands or suitors waiting at the bottom of the stairs. That seemed so impossible now as she viewed the gloom and the ice on the windows.

Still, she could almost see herself in a beautiful canary yellow gown and pearls around her neck, a silky fringed shawl hanging from the crooks of her elbows, and her hair in glossy curls piled high on her head. However, the only one at the bottom of the steps was the stout Winslow, carrying a silver tray with the mail.

He gave her a smile as she passed. "You're a ray of sunshine in this place, Mrs. Browning," he said. "Don't ever stop wearing bright colors and don't stop smiling that sunny smile."

She was surprised to hear Winslow speak in such

an easy manner, but she'd seen him sample the whiskey in the crystal bottle in the front parlor on various occasions, so mayhap she shouldn't be too surprised. Perhaps he drank whiskey to keep himself warm.

She wrapped her knitted shawl more closely around her and started filling the large four-armed candelabrum on the table in the foyer with candles. What the room needed was a welcoming fragrance. Perhaps she could get the children to pierce oranges with seeds of cloves to sweeten the air—if such extravagances were allowed in this household, she thought with a flash of bitterness.

Holly and mistletoe could be procured later for another hint of the celebrations to come.

She moved to the front parlor and filled all the candlesticks there. Pulling the drapes against the gloom, she longed to light the candles, but heaven forfend she would be caught doing something so out of the ordinary duties for a governess. She straightened a lace doily and arranged the candlesticks more attractively on the mantelpiece.

For a moment a longing for a home of her own came over her, but Matthew's pension was not enough to purchase a small house. By working, she would save and find a way to create a real home for Alex and herself somewhere.

In the green salon next door, she rearranged the carnations, chrysanthemums, and ferns that showed their glory to no one. On a whim, she moved the arrangement to the foyer and set it in the middle of the table. So much better, she thought. Whoever walked in would be cheered by the blooms.

The front door opened at that moment, and his lordship stepped inside, a few snowflakes melting on his shoulders. He stopped in his tracks as he removed his hat and stared at the flowers, then at her.

In her surprise, she clapped a hand to her open mouth and stared at him unblinkingly.

"What is going on here?" he asked suspiciously.

She took a deep breath. "I thought the beauty of these flowers was lost in the green salon. No one ever spends any time there—as far as I know."

"It was my wife's favorite room," he said stiffly.

"As I said, they shouldn't be wasted."

He shrugged his shoulders. One of the footmen took his hat and gloves and received his many-caped coat as he eased it off. He looked forbidding and handsome at the same time, the ends of his hair curling at the nape of his neck.

"You're taking on duties that aren't yours to have," he commented.

"I don't mind helping Mrs. Braithewaite now and again. She can't do everything on her own, and I enjoy decorating the halls for Christmas."

"We're not doing any decorations," he said without any inflection in his voice. He looked deadly serious, and Elinor wondered what had made him so bitter and so against the festivities.

"I understand if *you* don't have any desire to celebrate, but you're taking pleasure away from the children," she said. "I feel you have no right to do that."

"As outspoken as always," he said and crossed his arms over his chest. "Annie is too young to have any opinion on the matter, and if you desire to decorate your room for your son, I have no objections to that."

"That you would be against cheering for the holidays with your daughter is beyond me." She glanced around the cold foyer, where darkness had begun to creep into the corners as twilight descended outside. "This mansion needs a touch of joy. Children have a knack for bringing that to us more sober adults."

"I noticed you said 'us,'" he replied, his lip bending upward at the corner. "Very tactful of you."

"I have a fine line to walk."

"Which you have overstepped a number of times, Mrs. Browning."

"I'm not afraid to speak my mind if I believe it has merit."

"Even to the danger of losing your position? You have come precariously close, you know."

She stared into his dark eyes to see if he was jesting, but his expression was unreadable. The cynical side of her wondered if this man had ever smiled.

"I am not afraid to stand up for the truth."

"Then you would hardly make a good diplomat."

"I was never drawn to such work, my lord. Mayhap you were?" She didn't know what prompted her to goad him, but she couldn't stop herself. Her heartbeat had escalated alarmingly.

"Smoothing out tricky situations never appealed to me. If people don't have the ability to behave themselves with grace, I don't feel a need to teach them." He looked at her searchingly. "But I realize you might have the need to teach others what to do."

"That was as close to an insult as I've ever heard," she said. "Teaching is not something I chose with great joy, but I make sure I do my duty."

"You would rather apply your skills to flowers and candles," he said, including the arrangement and candle basket with the sweep of his arm.

She tweaked off a dead leaf. "I like beautiful things," she said noncommittally.

"How diplomatic of you."

This time she could see the faint smile playing over his lips.

She laughed. "I daresay." Taking the basket with her, she went to the sconces by the curving staircase and inserted tapers. "Light is what we need," she added. "Lots of light to lead us out of the gloom."

He stared at her, and as he walked across the marble and then the wood floor, the sound his Hessians made caused her stomach to flutter. The firm step was definitely masculine, and brooked no argument. "I don't know to what you're referring, Mrs. Browning."

She glanced around the foyer. "Take a good look, my lord. This is not a happy, light place."

"So I've been told many times, but I doubt a few candles are going to make a difference."

"You would be surprised. I don't mean to be critical, and I know it's not my place, but why don't you care?"

She watched him struggle with himself, as if debating whether to tell her the truth or deliver some inane excuse. "I . . . do care—sometimes—but this is the family pile, and nothing ever changes here."

"Somehow these flowers got here," she said and indicated the vase.

He nodded. "Someone sent them for my wife, Phoebe. Someone who didn't know she's dead. A friend from the past, *her* friend," he snapped, color rising above the collar of his shirt.

"'Tis odd a friend wouldn't know she'd passed."

"This person has been traveling in the East for the last two and a half years. An emissary of sorts."

A man, Elinor thought. She noted a storm cloud had gathered on the earl's forehead and knew there had been no warm feelings between Lord Lyons and this other man.

"He knows now, doesn't he?" she asked innocently.

He nodded. "Oh yes, he knows."

"That doesn't mean we shouldn't enjoy the beauty of these flowers as long as they last."

He pinched his lips together and gave the bouquet a contemptuous glance. "I ordered they be thrown away, but I gather my demand was ignored."

"'Twould have been a terrible waste," she replied. "Don't be upset with the servants. They long for cheer, too, and I advise you to bring in colors and scents for the festivities."

"You're all alike—nothing but demands and wishes."

"I take it you're speaking about the female species as a group?"

"Your irony is lost on me," he said icily. "I don't want to be connived or cajoled. It simply won't work on me. There's no game I don't see through."

"Who's speaking of games? Certainly not me. I'm speaking of sharing the beauty of these flowers."

He gave her a searching look, and his anger seemed to deflate.

"Conniving and manipulating take a lot of effort," she said, "I find it much easier to live by the simple truth."

She moved to a side table and placed some tapers in brass candlesticks.

He stepped across the floor and stared at the tapers she had just distributed. "They are words, Mrs. Browning. We all have big words to bandy about, but in actions we see the whole truth."

She turned to him, anger burning in her chest. "Then you shall have to judge for yourself. I don't feel any need to try to convince you. I have better things to do."

She hefted the basket and strode away from him and his icy stare. She didn't need to feel any colder than she already did.

Five

A few days later, Simon Nelson arrived at the mansion in Grosvenor Square to take Annie out shopping, which meant Elinor and Alex were going as well. They had dressed in their heaviest cloaks and hats, and the children wore colorful mittens Mrs. Braithewaite had knitted. Simon hoisted the little girl high in the air, and she squealed in delight.

"Cousin Simon, I'm flying! Look at me."

"You're my special songbird, Annie," he said with a happy smile. He set the girl down on the floor and smoothed down her velvet cloak. Then he patted Alex on the head.

"These are both fine children, don't you think, Elinor?"

She smiled. "I have to confess to being somewhat biased on the issue. Of course they are special and most blessed children."

"Come along, then." Simon lifted Annie's chin. "If you're that special, I shall buy you a paper cone filled with taffy. And mayhap we'll find the time to go to Gunther's for ices."

"Much too cold for ices, don't you think?" Elinor commented.

"'Tis never too cold for that," Simon said with a chuckle, and the children piped their approval.

Elinor glanced at Simon's rotund form and knew he would never turn away an opportunity to eat ices and other sweets.

"Will Papa come with us?" Annie asked. She glanced wistfully toward the door to the library.

"I doubt he has time for outings such as these," Elinor replied. "He is a very busy gentleman." She exchanged meaningful glances with Simon. His look seemed to imply she'd used too kindly a phrase, but she didn't want to speak ill of the earl in front of Annie.

Outside, ragged gray clouds scurried across a pale blue sky. The wind felt biting against her face, and she cherished the freshness after the gloomy morning inside the house.

Simon assisted them into his coach and ordered the driver to take them to Bond Street. They arrived in high spirits and stepped into the grimy snow outside the shops. The children immediately wanted to make snowballs, but Elinor marched them into the nearest shop that sold books and elegant writing implements.

She admonished the little ones to behave themselves, but knew they were in too high spirits to last very long in a shop that offered few items of interest to them.

She admired a beautiful ink bottle with an ornate hinged silver lid. The bottle and a goose quill holder stood on a marble base. "Isn't it lovely?" she asked.

"For those who write, maybe," Simon said. He strolled down the aisle of books, touching a spine here and there.

She loved the scent of vellum and leather, but it was evident he had scant interest in printed matter.

"There's a lot of talk about Sir Walter Scott's latest publication, *Waverly*," Elinor said. "Did you read it, Simon?"

He shook his head. "The newspaper is the extent of my reading material. And playbills. I love the theater."

Elinor sighed. "I haven't attended the theater for a long time, and in my present situation, I'm hardly likely to."

"I'll take you, dear Elinor!" Simon cried.

"You'd be ostracized by the sticklers for propriety, Simon."

"I don't care. You have an impeccable lineage."

"Be that as it may, I'm no longer a lady of leisure." Elinor lovingly touched the cover of a book, realizing she didn't have money to spend on unnecessary items. She had to save for the future and Alex's education.

"'Tis a pity none of your kin has an inclination to assist you." Simon gave her a searching stare. "It must be deuced uncomfortable to be a poor relation."

"My cousins regret that they can't take care of me." Elinor smiled. "I'm never bored, mind you. I enjoy using my wits."

"You have plenty of those," he replied with a chuckle.

The door opened, sending a gust of icy air through the shop. Elinor noted from the corner of her eye that a gentleman in a drab greatcoat had stepped inside.

"Even though we're distant relations, I have a mind to make a play for your heart," Simon continued. "Just to have your delightful company at all times."

Elinor laughed. "You're so kind, Simon, but you know we would never suit."

He didn't look too put out. "Your laugh is like a rippling brook."

Someone loomed over her shoulder, and she realized her banter with Simon had been overheard.

"Where's my daughter?" a deep male voice said in her ear.

She whirled around, her heart beating faster. Lord Lyons stared into her eyes, and she couldn't find her breath for a moment. Even as she opened her mouth, the children came running around the corner and Annie yelled, "Papa! You came after all. I'm so glad, and so is Mrs. Browning!"

Lord Lyons's deep eyes held a question as he kept Elinor's gaze trapped. Something, a tingling sensation, passed between them, and Elinor swallowed hard.

Annie stopped right at the earl's feet, not daring to touch him. She glanced up at him with longing in her eyes, and Elinor sensed her pain.

She prayed that the earl would swing Annie into his arms, but he didn't move.

"I saw your carriage at Grosvenor Square, Simon, and Mrs. Braithewaite told me you'd gone out with the children." He sent his cousin a guarded look. She was sure he'd overheard her conversation with Simon.

"We're enjoying an outing, even if the weather does not invite people to step outside," Simon said with a big grin. "Elinor needs a change of scenery sometimes so as not to wither away in that dark mansion of yours. I feel somewhat responsible for her, as I was the one to push for her employment. Possibly a mistake," he said with a grimace, "but only in the sense that she has to put up with you, Lucas."

"I like Mrs. Browning," Annie piped up. She gave Elinor an adoring glance, and Elinor bent down and gave the girl a hug.

"I like you too, Annie."

"And *I* do, Annie," Simon chimed in. "You're my favorite, and always will be. When you grow up I shall marry you."

Annie giggled and Alex groaned in disgust.

"I distinctly overheard another proposition as I stepped up to greet you," the earl said coldly.

"I am a flighty fellow, what can I say?" Simon replied with a nonchalant shrug of his shoulders. He spread his arms to Annie and she ran to him with a squeal.

Alex clung to Elinor's hand and stared at the earl

with suspicion. "We don't have to go home yet, do we, Mama?"

"No . . . not yet." Elinor felt embarrassed that Alex would call the mansion in Grosvenor Square home, but it was true. He knew no other home.

"Are you coming along, Lucas?" Simon asked. "'Tis the least you can do now that you've found us."

"I daresay you can't be trusted with the ladies' virtue," the earl said drily.

"It's the first witticism I've heard from you in a long time, old fellow. It's about time."

"Why don't you bare my whole life story for everyone to hear, Simon?"

"It wouldn't hurt to air out the closets," Simon said carelessly. "You've brooded much too long."

The earl's pale cheeks turned red, and Elinor noted the fire in his dark eyes. She was glad Simon, not she, had crossed him.

"Cousin, I didn't ask for your advice." His voice couldn't be colder.

"And if you're thinking of planting me a facer, I have to ask you to refrain until a more convenient moment." He hugged Annie closer.

"What's a facer?" she asked timidly.

"Something gentlemen do to each other when they are angry."

"Are you angry with Papa?"

"Sometimes," Simon said baldly. "Your papa is a very stubborn man."

Annie seemed to mull it over. "Is that good?"

"It depends on what you're stubborn about."

The earl's face looked ever more thunderous. "You must be about in your head, Simon, to fill the girl's ears with such drivel."

"'Tis only the truth, Lucas."

"Papa, I've been promised sweetmeats." Annie looked at her father expectantly. "Cousin Simon will buy you some if you ask kindly. Bonbons will make you happy, don't you think?"

Elinor could not stop herself from laughing. She wondered if the earl would soften, but he didn't even smile. Clearly flustered, he said as he gazed at the rack of books, "No, Annie. I don't care for bonbons."

Annie looked disappointed and hid her face in Simon's shoulder. Elinor's hand itched to slap the earl, but that would only make matters worse. What *did* he care for?

"Well, let's continue our stroll," Simon said cheerfully. "You haven't changed your mind about joining us, have you, Lucas?" His voice demanded that the earl join the group, and the man had the look of a trapped animal. He nodded curtly.

"I came to buy a book . . . very well. If you insist."

"I do."

Alex gripped Simon's one hand, Annie the other. As they walked ahead on the street, carefully staying away from the slush sprayed by carriage wheels, Elinor hung back with the earl. Out of earshot of the others, she berated in a low, heated voice, "You could've improved matters with Annie immensely if you'd agreed with her—even if you don't like bonbons."

"I—"

"I don't care for your excuses! You're the most obstinate, shortsighted man I've ever clapped eyes on. And the most egotistical. What has Annie ever done to you to deserve your rejection? She needs to be hugged."

"I—"

"She's just a little girl who looks to you for love and support, and all you can think about are your own desires and preferences. Haven't you learned to put your child first in your life?" She wanted to shout at the top of her lungs to vent her anger further, but the urge was a fleeting one.

His eyes were hooded as he glanced at her. "I daresay you treat all your employers with such outspoken contempt."

"Only if their behavior warrants it."

"And mine does?"

She pulled her cloak more closely around her as the wind threatened to dislodge it. "You're the most difficult and truculent individual I've ever come upon."

His low voice trembled with anger. "You appoint yourself as judge and jury at every turn."

"I'm Annie's champion. No more, no less." She stared him square in the eye.

"And flawless, no doubt."

"That goes without saying," she retorted without missing a breath. She glanced at him, her blood boiling, but even as she spoke the words, she wanted to laugh out loud.

She doubted he would see the humor, but his

lips twitched at the corners, surprising her. He would look so handsome if he smiled fully, she thought.

People around them laughed as they walked by a nearby milliner's shop, but the laughter seemed far away. Elinor was aware only of the earl's close proximity.

"Do you share the Christmas cheer?" she asked to say something.

"On Bond Street? The only cheer here is the clink of coin in the shop owners' cash boxes."

Elinor looked around at the pine-bedecked windows and doors, and the shoppers laden with parcels and baskets. Candlelight glowed invitingly in the windows, dispelling the gloom of the overcast day. "You're missing the point if all you see is the profit."

"And everyone contributing to it," he added, but there was a teasing glint in his eyes.

"Are you accusing me of being a spendthrift?" she goaded back.

"On a governess's wages, I doubt you can spend a great deal."

"Then I hope you'll give me and the other servants Christmas bonuses so I can buy something special for Alex at yule time," she said boldly. "He adores chocolate."

"I suspect his mother does, too."

"On . . . occasion," she replied with a smile.

"Only on occasion? You'll not bamboozle me, Mrs. Browning." He looked disgusted for a moment, but then let it go.

She sensed he didn't have a lot of trust in women, possibly suspecting her of an ulterior motive if she showed her wit or her joy. "And I have no reason to trifle with you, my lord. I mean what I say."

"And you don't have any problem voicing your opinion, whether it's solicited or not." He took her elbow and steered her out of harm's way of a frisky horse.

His grip made her aware of his male strength, and she felt comforted. She stumbled briefly on a clump of snow and fell against him. His arm came around her shoulders as he steadied her.

"Oh . . . I'm sorry," she said, her face feeling hot.

"Don't mention it," he replied curtly. As if being cautious, he stepped away from her, his face closed, but she noticed the startled look he gave her. He hadn't been totally oblivious to her closeness.

"No need to apologize," he added stiffly.

For a moment she couldn't find anything to say, and he kept silent, too. In unspoken consent, they hurried forward until they caught up with Simon and the children.

"Alex!" Elinor admonished as the child kept pulling Simon in the direction of a shop filled with carved toys. A rocking horse in the window held Annie's complete attention. Her face glowed with enchantment.

"Look, Papa." She pointed at the horse, which had been painted brown with intricate and colorful details on the saddle and the tackle. "Isn't she beautiful?"

"She?" the earl asked.

"Of course it's a 'she'," Simon filled in. "Just look at the flirtatious look in her eye and the dainty hooves. 'Tis certainly not a stallion."

The earl gave Simon an angry look.

"I can't say I see any kind of flirtation in her eye," Elinor admonished.

"It takes a gentleman to appreciate it." Simon laughed.

"You must be touched in your upper works, Coz, or you looked too deeply into the brandy bottle."

"Must've been the Blue Ruin I had for breakfast, old fellow."

Alex kept pulling at Simon's hand. "Look! There's a whole stable of carved animals." He pointed at the back corner of the small window.

Elinor wondered how anyone could carve such tiny animals. She would come back another time and find out if her purse could afford the stable for Alex.

Annie stood with her nose pressed to the window, her face still rapt. Elinor glanced at the earl, who stared at the people walking by, as if paying no attention to Annie.

If the man had any kind of human compassion in his cold heart, he would make arrangements to surprise the child with the gift of the rocking horse. She gave him a withering stare, and his eyes narrowed. Clearly he caught her unspoken suggestion to attend to his daughter, but he chose to ignore it. *A regular cod's head*, she thought uncharitably. She never could abide unfeeling gentlemen.

"Alex, enough's enough." She hauled the boy away from the window, then gripped Annie's hand and urged her along. Without another word she headed back to Simon's carriage at the end of the street. She heard the men following, but at this moment she had no patience with them.

It was one thing to be ignorant and innocent, but to be a complete blockhead like the earl was the outside of enough!

She didn't know if she could remain in his employ for much longer.

Six

That night, a flash of light awakened Lucas, a flash so bright it blinded him. At first he thought it had appeared in a dream, but he touched the velvet hangings on his bed and felt the softness. The room was very cold and dark. The fire must've gone out and no one had thought to light another. He could barely see the transparent windowpanes against the deeper blackness of the walls.

His eyes gritty, he stared into the gloom. At first, nothing happened, but then a glow brightened in the corner. The light had an unearthly quality, which could penetrate the deepest darkness without difficulty. It kept growing, and the earl shied back in fear. He rubbed his eyes with cold knuckles and shivered. Church bells in the distance tolled once, morosely and woefully.

When he opened his eyes again, the glow hovered right by the bed, and he felt his chest tighten with apprehension.

"Father?" he asked, wondering if the same apparition would manifest out of the light. The glow seemed to fill the entire space of his four-poster bed, and at first he could see a faint outline of a man, this one short and thick, with long muscular arms. Sparks seemed to shoot out of his skin.

The vision sat down on the edge of the bed and stared at him with kind eyes that might've been blue. He wasn't sure. There was no mistaking the glowing halo around his head and the ever youthful face, though he somehow knew the ghost was old.

"Who are you?" Lucas finally managed to ask as he tried desperately to wake up from this nightmare.

"The Ghost of Christmas Past," the apparition said, not unkindly. Every word brought more sparks, this time flying from his mouth.

"What do you want with me?"

"To reclaim the man you once were, you must observe the past."

"I have no idea what you're talking about," Lucas said, his whole body frozen as if ice water flowed through his veins.

The ghost held out a strong-looking hand that seemed to undulate as he moved. It might look strong, but also insubstantial, Lucas thought. There could be no real strength in it—or could there?

"I'm here to show you the truth."

"I don't need to be shown anything," Lucas replied, now angry.

"Your father warned you of total desolation if you don't change. Do you want that to happen? You have a choice presently, and you'd better make the right one."

The earl looked at the smiling ghost, and he reached out to touch the extended arm, but his hand completely disappeared in the glow. With a gasp, he pulled away. The ghostly glow had a crystal clear quality and a coldness to match, and he wasn't sure if he could handle such sharp clarity.

"What do you want from me?" he asked, putting his hand under his armpit to warm it.

"A willingness to look at the truth. I think you have it now, if you didn't earlier. We shall take a journey through time."

Just as Lucas opened his mouth to protest, the ghost reached out and put his hand in the area of the earl's heart. Lucas had the odd sensation of lifting from his bed, but he swore he hadn't moved. His nightshirt fell around his calves and the floor touched the bottom of his feet with ice. The ghost's hand closed around his arm.

The next thing he knew, they were outside, flying over London. Smoke rose from hundreds of chimney pots, and stars glistened in the distant dome above. A fog—not unpleasant—folded around him, and he lost his perception of direction.

A steadying sensation came over him, and the fog stopped rolling around him. He felt ground under his feet again, and he stared upon a familiar scene: Lyons Court in Kent, the family seat where he'd grown up.

The day was cold and clear, the trees leafless and unmoving in the still winter air. Smoke curled silver gray against the pale blue sky, and he was transported inside.

A small girl not much younger than Annie, with bouncing brown curls and rosy cheeks, came rushing toward him across the ancient paneled hall: Edith, his little sister who had died suddenly when she was six. She'd been so full of joy. He'd forgotten how much he'd loved her, and how protective he'd felt about her.

She smelled of ripe apples. She'd loved to pick apples in the fall. A myriad of scents of simple joys floated toward him: pies baking, the way fish smelled down by the river when he'd caught them with his fishing pole, autumn leaves burning, the leather of new shoes, the scratchy feel of wool against his skin. He'd hated wool with a passion. How could it itch so much when sheep were so soft?

He remembered the love and kindness of the old retainers who'd lived and served at Lyons Court all their lives. When his parents had failed in their support, there had always been someone to wipe a tear and to wash a scraped knee.

"What is it that I see on your face? A tender smile?" the ghost asked and touched his arm anew. A bird, wings spreading inside him, opened his chest, and a mixture of pain and joy flowed out. He longed to bend down and feel the earth and cry.

The ghost took him by the hand, and they walked into the back of the mansion, where a fire burned in the parlor. His mother sat stiffly in her chair, focusing on an embroidery frame in front of her. A stillness lay over her, a kind of peace, but Lucas could see her loneliness like a heavy mantle on her shoulders. He saw right into her heart, and read the pain in what she'd lost.

In the library sat his father, stooped over a book

he wasn't even reading. The pages never turned, and his father's eyes looked cold and distant, as if he was seeing only the bitter memories of the past. Though the house lacked no fires or other comforts, there was a chill in the air that comes from heavy emotions and the lack of people talking. Words were never spoken, but sat like tiny malevolent ghosts in the air around his parents.

He wanted to cry even as his mother's tears soiled the fabric of her embroidery.

The ghost led him upstairs, where the air held a distinct chill. Loneliness filled the silent corridors and empty chambers. Dust was the only thing that moved as they passed through. They floated through a wall into a small chamber where a boy sat clad in a beautiful jacket and knee breeches, as befitted a young gentleman.

But what was the occasion? A single candle burned on the mantelpiece, and Lucas read dejection in the child's slumped shoulders.

He shuddered as he recognized himself as that boy. The burden of neglect, much too heavy for someone that young, lay over him. Where Edith would've been a companion, he had no one else. His missing her sat like a lead weight in his chest—but here she was, right beside him, bouncing up and down without a care in the world.

"A sad little boy, weren't you?" the ghost said, and he nodded.

A knock on the door came, and an old servant entered. "Nanny Gibbins," Lucas cried. "I'd forgotten that kind soul."

"You've forgotten everything except your bitterness," the ghost said.

"She's carrying something." Lucas watched intently as the old woman brought a parcel that had been tied with old wrinkled paper and red string. On a plate she carried a slice of rum cake, a currant bun, and an assortment of cookies. She even handed the boy a glass of mulled wine.

"'Twill warm your insides." She patted young Lucas's shoulder with a gnarled hand. "'Tis a shame you'd be sittin' here all alone on Christmas Day." She stroked his hair tenderly, and he remembered the feel of her awkward hands that had soothed him so many times when he had no one. He recalled her kind peppercorn eyes and her wheezy laughter at some prank he'd perpetrated.

"Nanny Gibbins never had an angry word to say to me."

"She knew you were getting those aplenty from other sources. Your father never had a kind word for you, did he?"

Lucas remembered the bitter man in the library and felt the chasm that had always been there widen. He'd always told himself his father never had an easy life with so many relatives dying in the family, but truth to tell, Lucas couldn't well remember any of them. They had never been a close family.

The death of Edith had been the worst of all experiences. He could bear the outbursts and bruises of his father's anger, but had he in some way been guilty of bringing on Edith's death?

As if in response, the ghost brought him through the walls and outside to a pond, where terror struck him. Edith had almost drowned before she'd died in that fever. He could see it so clearly, as if it were yesterday.

They had been playing outside, chasing the dogs. Edith's new pug puppy had run into the mud at the edge of the pond and sunk more deeply with its frantic efforts to get out. Edith had gone in after it, through the water, and had also gotten stuck in the mud.

Help had arrived, of course. The servants always kept a close watch. Old Mike Neddy, one of the grooms, had sworn to Lucas's father that Lucas had not instigated the adventure, the dog had.

It had been the truth, but Lucas's father had never forgotten the incident, or gotten over Edith's death, and Lucas had borne a great burden of guilt. He felt its weight now, but it lightened miraculously as the ghost swept a glowing arm around his shoulders.

The scene faded completely, and so did Edith, waving and laughing as they floated on the air.

The fog enveloped him again, and they landed in a town in the heart of England. Oxford. He'd been banished there, away from sad and accusing parental eyes. Freedom from oppression, but swift punishment every time he executed any kind of rebellion. It was worse hell to return to Lyons Court than it was to behave at Oxford, no matter how suffocating the education had been.

"I don't want to see this," he said to the ghost, who hung at his elbow.

"Too painful, is it?"

Lucas hung his head. "Yes . . . I suppose it is."

"The pain is like the icicles on the roof. It melts in the sun."

Lucas peered at the ghost. "I've never thought of it that way." He closed his eyes, shutting out the picture of the college where he'd never fit in. "I could never play and drink like my contemporaries did at college," he said. "A most boring fellow, they called me."

"You took interest in learning about the running of great estates, something that is admirable as long as there's a happy purpose to it," the ghost replied kindly. "Somehow you got lost in the work as an excuse not to look at the other areas of your life."

Lucas was going to protest, but he couldn't find any words. In fact, his voice had disappeared altogether, and he knew it was the ghost's doing.

The next moment they flew through the air, and he found himself back in his bedchamber at the mansion in Grosvenor Square. The room still remained cold and uninviting, but he felt solid wood under his feet, and he could draw a breath of relief that he'd been safely returned to familiar surroundings.

He glanced around the room, and everything lay in darkness. Not the faintest glow could be seen anywhere, but he heard a voice he recognized as the ghost's.

"The sorrows of Christmases past don't have to be brought into this time. Lighten your burdens. You're the only one who carries them. Loneliness is your own choice. Friends are always around you whether you care to look for them or not."

The voice faded as the words hung in the air, and Lucas felt curiously light-headed. He didn't want to let the thousands of thoughts racing about his mind take over. He sought his bed as if nothing untoward had happened to him.

Lucas stared at the velvet canopy, but could not focus on anything that soothed him into a sleepy mode. How could he, after such an experience? His world literally had been torn apart.

The church bells clanged mournfully—only once—and it startled him. He must've been out with the ghost for hours, so why did the bell strike one again? He had no explanation.

He tossed and turned in bed, feeling as if he were hanging by a thread from the ceiling. The sensation of being out of control bothered him, and he swung his legs over the side of the mattress and buried his face in his hands.

His feelings chafed raw within. The ghost had brought up things he didn't want to remember, but they had always been there. He couldn't deny the events had happened as they had.

Sighing, he got up and lighted the candles on his bedstand. If only there were some sounds to distract him. Wide awake, he decided to go downstairs and look for something to eat in the larder. Sleep always came much easier on a full stomach, and for some reason he was famished.

He picked up a candlestick and went down the curving stairway. No one halted his progress, and he stepped toward the kitchen. The mansion sat in complete gloom, and he wondered if the sun would ever shine through the hallway windows again.

Of course it would, he scoffed to himself. It had before.

He went to the kitchen, where a fire still glowed in the grate. The air carried a distinct warmth, and he reveled in it as it chased away the iciness of his lonely existence abovestairs.

He found a mold of pork and a slab of ham, from which he cut a heavy slice. A crock of mustard offered up spice for the ham. In the bread bin, he discovered slices of bread, fresh from this morning no doubt, and sugared buns on a plate covered with a pristine white napkin. Cook had left everything meticulous, and he sliced a plum cake with great care so as not to leave crumbs everywhere. He would never hear the end of it from Cook if he did.

The scents of cinnamon, ripe plums, raisins, and flour filled the air, and he inhaled deeply, finding the smells oddly comforting.

He carried his food on a plate to the kitchen, where the fire still smoldered in the huge hearth. This was the only truly warm room in the mansion, and he sat down as close to the fire as he could. His limbs felt stiff and heavy, as if carrying the weight of centuries.

He refused to dwell on the experience he'd had with the ghost. *Damn! I don't even believe in ghosts!*

But he couldn't deny the raw emotions surging in his chest. He'd forgotten the pain of his childhood, as some ugly vase pushed to the back of a cupboard but never brought out. The only reason it was still there was that Aunt Amelia had given it to him a long time ago.

He chewed on a piece of cake but couldn't taste it. His heart felt as if an old wound, healed on the surface, had reopened.

The sound of a closing door brought him to the present, and he turned around and came eye to eye with Mrs. Browning, who was dressed in a huge mobcap and an old dressing gown of some lavender material with embroideries. In fact, she looked quite fetching in her dishabille.

She had a guilty expression on her face as she found him, and she pulled her gown more closely together, as if he could see something that would embarrass her—or him—under the voluminous folds.

"Oh, I'm sorry. I didn't know you were here," she said lamely. "I don't want to intrude."

"You're not intruding," he said, and was actually grateful for her appearance. She brought normalcy to this strange situation.

She held up a glass pitcher as if to show why she was roaming around in the middle of the night. "I'm thirsty, and this is empty."

"No need to explain. I'm certain you didn't have in mind to steal the plum cake."

"Do I detect an unexpected hint of humor?" She walked to the pump in the adjoining scullery and filled her pitcher.

He didn't respond, not even sure why he'd joked about the cake. He didn't have a desire to joke.

When she returned, he said, "Do you want a piece of cake or something else?"

She stared at him for a long moment, perhaps sensing his loneliness. "Yes . . . mayhap. Cook's cakes are the best in London," she said and went to cut herself a piece in the larder.

She pulled up a stool next to the fire, so close to the earl that their knees almost touched.

She pulled away self-consciously, but she yearned for the warmth of the fire.

He noted the brush of the fabric of her gown against his, a curiously intimate sensation, and for a fleeting moment he wished she'd lingered close.

"I see you have a good appetite even at this ungodly hour," she said.

He nodded and smiled wryly. "'Tis late and I haven't slept a wink. Food might be helpful."

She smiled uncertainly and broke off a piece of cake with her fingertips. He noticed how sensitive her slim fingers looked. She appeared much softer than normal, as if the late hour blurred her features and smoothed out all lines.

"Do you suffer from insomnia often?" she asked as she chewed daintily.

He shook his head. "Only lately." He studied her earnest face, and before he could stop himself, he blurted out, "I saw a ghost tonight."

"A ghost?"

"'Tis not the first time."

She smiled fully now. "I'm not surprised. Is it someone you know? One of your ancestors?"

"You find humor in this?"

"No. I believe every mansion has its ghosts."

"You do? Well, I didn't believe—until lately."

She didn't reply, only stared thoughtfully into the fire.

"It would be very hard for me to believe if my own eyes hadn't . . ." He heaved a deep sigh and let the words trail off.

"Did it clump around, making a lot of noise?"

He shook his head. "No. He came and fetched me to witness the past. He was the Ghost of Christmas Past. We actually walked through the walls without encountering any resistance."

"Oh."

"You must think I'm a complete mawworm."

"No." Her expression looked sincere.

"He came with the purpose of showing me the error of my ways."

"Were you frightened?" she asked, her face glowing slightly orange from the dying fire.

He made a grimace. "'Twould be a lie to say the opposite."

"It makes you human," she said with a tiny smile.

"I gather I've been an ogre for a long time."

"I didn't say that, did I?"

"I heard the underlying accusation."

"Only if you're looking for that. 'Tis your cynicism speaking, my lord. You're a bitter man."

He set down his plate on the floor at his feet. "You're not the first person to point that out," he said.

"And probably not the last one." She grinned as she broke off another piece of cake.

"I find no hilarity in that comment."

"Tell me about the ghost."

He almost regretted having brought up the subject, but he needed to share the experience with someone.

He retold every detail he could remember, from the moment the ghost had appeared at his bed. "I didn't recall how difficult life was since Edith, my sister, died." He looked at her to see if she expressed sympathy or disgust. She appeared more surprised than anything. "I'm not looking for pity. The experience shook me to the marrow."

"So I would imagine. To what purpose did it happen?"

"To help me change." He hung his head, too weary to hold it up. "I must have windmills in my head to share these strange events with you."

"Under normal circumstances you wouldn't tell me anything, so something must've happened to open you up in this way. I do believe you saw that apparition, and it might be a good thing."

He decided to tell her about his father's ghost, and realized he needed to share the event. It had hung as a burden on his shoulders ever since it happened. "The first ghost to appear, the other week, was my father. His manifestation was completely unexpected. We were never close in life. In fact, no man could've been colder and more sour than he. I resented feeling so much anger toward him, but I understand nothing could've made him happy. He fought every effort of others to reach him. My sister was the only ray of sunshine in that house," he murmured, "and once she was gone, everything was gone. My father loved her beyond words."

They sat in silence for a long while, and he wanted to talk about so many things, but didn't know where to start. He also feared she wasn't willing to listen to any more dirges. He slanted a glance at her, and she had a faraway look in her eyes.

She set down her plate absentmindedly on the brick ledge in the hearth. "I was more fortunate in my parents, then. I remember my father as kind and wise. We shared a lot of jollities in our house— garden parties, evenings of watercolor painting, pianoforte exercises, dance classes, lively discussions, and penny card games. Not to mention riding in the meadows and collecting flowers for drying."

"Sounds very innocent."

"Certainly. And very enjoyable. 'Twas very sad when my parents passed on to their heavenly rewards. My sister Evelyn married a clergyman in Kent, and they have five children. Happy but poor, and it doesn't matter because they have each other and their love."

He slowly turned his head, a massive effort. He'd never felt so tired. "You believe . . . that they are . . . truly happy?" For some reason he desperately wanted to believe, and his attention hung on her lips as they formed the word.

"Yes."

"You're so innocent, Mrs. . . . Br—Elinor." He thought the name over silently. "'Tis a beautiful name—Elinor. Do you mind my calling you by your given name?"

She chuckled. "Not at all, *my lord*," she said.

"Lucas."

She repeated the name, and he could barely hear her voice. He wanted to hear her say it aloud, but could hardly demand it.

"I'm not that innocent. I have been married, if you recall, and mine was a happy marriage, even though I didn't see enough of Matthew. Then he passed on. Life isn't very fair, is it? We never had a chance to grow old together."

"I don't even comprehend what that would be like," he said, a wave of bitterness coming over him. "'Tis an outlandish idea, one no one thinks about on their wedding day."

They looked at each other, and he wondered what she'd looked like on her wedding day. For a fleeting moment he experienced jealousy of the man who had gained her love, but look where it had ended.

"The fire is dying," she said simply and pointed to the glowing embers.

Without a word he put more wood on, and small flames leaped around the logs. Soon more warmth spread around their ankles.

"The kitchen is the heart of a house, don't you agree?" she asked. "We're not supposed to be here. Cook would be very upset if she found us."

He chortled. "You have to remember 'tis my house, Elinor."

"The master of the house *never* appears below-stairs."

"I may be traditional, but I'm not above creating some new habits."

"I won't tell anyone."

"I will not slink about my house like a thief in the night, Elinor. I don't care if the whole world knows."

"Then we shall tell everyone I sat here for hours dishabille with you in the night."

He smiled. "Your reputation will be forever ruined."

"Be that as it may, I'm not very worried. I'm not a society miss searching for an advantageous match." She stood, smoothing out her dressing gown. Clearly, she looked a bit discomfited as she thought about their situation.

"Thank you for lending an ear to my strange tales. I think I can now bear the thought that I met a ghost tonight."

"More than one, I'd say. You met the ghosts of your past, whether you like it or not."

He stood and looked down at her earnest, open face. "You're right, but to what purpose?"

"You might discover a more compassionate side to your character."

"Compassion equals softness to me, an invitation to new hurts."

"Love does not hurt. Lack of love does."

He stared into her face for a long moment, longing deep in his heart. Mesmerized, he couldn't look away.

Seven

His face kept coming closer to hers, and his hands gripped her shoulders. She could feel their warmth through the fabric, and the strength of his grip.

He pulled her closer and his breath wafted softly over her hair. She held her own breath as his mouth came down to cover hers in a kiss of such tender longing that she felt light-headed with surprise.

She had always looked at the earl as an utterly hard man, but his lips explored hers with such soft warmth that she nearly melted. As the kiss grew more insistent and he pressed her close to himself, she suspected she would've crumpled at his feet if he hadn't held her upright.

He must've come to realize the impropriety of the situation and pulled back. His eyes locked with hers, unfocused and dazed, and she wasn't sure she could ever find her voice again.

"I . . . sorry," he whispered. "I don't know what came over me. Desperation, perhaps."

He gently released her, and she grabbed the back of a chair to steady herself.

"I have no desire to embarrass you," he continued. He raked his hands through his hair. "Please forget my trespass."

She pressed her fingertips to her lips, feeling her blood pounding through her body. "I . . . you . . . I don't know what happened." She didn't want to examine her feelings too closely. Kissing the earl had been an unthinkable act.

"Again, I apologize. 'Twill never happen again."

"We were both vulnerable," she said lamely. Relieved and disappointed at the same time, she wondered how she'd ever face the earl again after this. They would both remember, and he would recall he'd shared some very intimate memories with her, which gave her a certain power over him. She could read the uncertainty and the unspoken question in his eyes: would she share what he'd told her with the others in the household?

"Don't worry, my lord. I'll keep your confidence. I understand you needed to talk to someone." She managed a smile. "It's not always one runs into two ghosts in such a short period of time."

"You're right." His lips quirked at the corners. "Quite startling. I hate to admit I was frightened, but it's unsettling to find oneself without control."

"I trust something good will come out of it. They were good spirits, not ghouls from the dungeons."

He laughed. "We don't have dungeons here, thank God."

She smiled back, sensing a lifting of her mood as if on wings. It had been a long time since she felt so light. "It has been an edifying night, to say the least."

They cleaned up the remnants of their forage into the larder and put the plates in the scullery.

"There, the proof of our stealth has been removed," he said. "No one can accuse us of any crime."

"Cook will wonder what happened to a large portion of her plum cake."

"She can't prove our guilt. Besides, we can always blame it on the cat." He pointed at the black feline curled up on one of the chairs.

"He has the reputation of a good mouser, so I doubt he's interested in cake," she replied drily.

The earl caught her hand and kissed it. "Good night, and thank you for listening. May the rest of your night be peaceful."

She blushed and watched as he left the room, his stride filled with its usual assurance. Lifting the full water pitcher, she went back to her room. The coldness enveloped her and she curled up under the quilts on her bed and pulled them up around her ears.

The hour was late when she finally fell asleep, and she dreamed of kissing the earl in a meadow full of summer flowers with the children laughing in the background. She recalled the dream when she awakened, and knew it would never become reality.

The earl had not slept, even though he'd been exhausted. The morning dawned gray and wintry, the ragged clouds chasing each other across the sky. He could not put the ghost out of his mind, nor could he tear his thoughts away from Elinor's sweet mouth. He could still remember every nuance of her, and a tingle traveled through him from head to toe. Damn it all.

It just wouldn't do to spend his time thinking about Annie's governess in any way except as the servant he paid to look after Annie.

"Blast and damn," he muttered to himself as he marched to the library to do some work.

Ian Brinkley already sat at his ledgers. From sunrise to sunset, he worked diligently to take care of Lucas's affairs. *I could never find a more reliable fellow,* he thought.

"Good morning, my lord," Brinkley said with a smile. "Isn't it wonderful?"

"You're the eternal optimist," the earl said with his customary dourness.

"Life truly is wonderful most of the time. I see no reason to complain."

Lucas shook his head and sat down at his desk. He looked over a stack of letters on the blotter, everything in complete order. "You're always perfect, Brinkley. Don't you ever make any mistakes? Don't you ever get up on the wrong side of the bed?"

The secretary shook his head. "No. I'm grateful for my fortune. There are so many who are not able to eat a hot meal every day."

"That reminds me. Remember those people who came and asked for alms some weeks ago?"

The steward nodded. "Yes."

"I now regret that I didn't support them with a contribution. Christmas is coming, and some efforts at charity would not hurt."

Brinkley stared at him for a long moment, his eyes narrowing as if he struggled to understand this new turn of events. "Your concern commends you, my lord."

"Find them and make a contribution to the shelter. A hundred pounds, I think."

Brinkley's mouth fell open.

"You look like a fish out of water, Brinkley. You heard me right. There's no need to be stingy. We can't bring monetary wealth into heaven."

Brinkley still did not respond. The goose quill fell to the pages on the table in front of him.

"Mayhap it is a strange sentiment to be expressed, Brinkley, but people can change, you know."

Brinkley gripped his goose quill with sudden force, as if dazed with shock. He stuck it into the ink pot and gathered his papers. An angelic smile spread on his face. "I shall see to it, my lord. Right this moment. You're very kind to think of those starving in the streets."

"I knew you would approve," the earl said sardonically.

He signed the letters and studied the ledgers. The rest of the time he stared out the window across the room, where another gray day was traveling on its gloomy way from morning to midday. Hunger drove him to the dining room at noon, and he found the servants had put out a tureen of fish and potato soup, cold cuts, and delicious-smelling bread. It still felt warm to the touch as he tested it, remembering his nocturnal tryst with Elinor.

A sharp stab of longing went through him.

He called to Winslow, the butler, as one of the footmen served him a bowl of soup.

"Please fetch Mrs. Browning. Nanny Wendell can look after the children for a few minutes."

The butler bowed and went to execute the order. Elinor entered five minutes later, the fresh fragrance of lavender and warm womanhood around her. Lucas realized he'd missed her since they'd parted in the night.

"Good afternoon, Mrs. Browning," he said, addressing her formally for the benefit of the other servants in the room.

"You wanted to see me, my lord?" she greeted with a cool smile.

She looked pale and distraught, he thought. "Would you like to share the midday meal with me? I'd like to hear about the progress in the schoolroom." He realized the excuse was feeble, and he saw the error too late. Blast and thunder, he *should* take interest in Annie's progress.

She studied him as if debating whether to turn down the offer or obey. She couldn't very well reject him, but after what had happened last night, he would have to be prepared to accept her rejection. Truly, she had more power over him than she knew.

"Thank you, my lord."

The footmen arranged another place setting and she sat down. The shiny vastness of the table stretched the length of the dining room, and they seemed tethered on an island by themselves at one end.

"The soup is delicious," he said lamely.

"I'm sure Cook has outdone herself as always," Elinor said noncommittally.

He smiled. "I don't see any plum cake," he said, glancing at the sideboard.

"Someone must've finished it off," she said, her eyes twinkling.

He relaxed. She wasn't angry or nervous, only properly reserved, as was any servant at the mansion when he addressed them.

He watched as she spooned soup daintily into her mouth. She had a fine, straight nose, and a full mouth he so vividly remembered kissing.

"You called me down to speak of Annie," she reminded him as she patted her lips with the linen napkin.

"How is she doing?"

"She has a very bright and curious mind and is already beginning to read. She knows her alphabet and is proud of it. I suspect she'll be one to find great pleasures in reading as she grows up."

"I see."

"It should be encouraged, my lord."

He nodded and couldn't stop himself from teasing Elinor. "Yes, she may read for me in my old age," he said.

"More than that, I hope!" she replied heatedly. "She may become a writer like Miss Austen."

"There's always that," he said drily, knowing he was tugging at her strings.

She put her chin in the air. "An admirable woman, Miss Austen."

"Most admirable."

"Lord Lyons, I believe you're not serious at all." She lowered her voice. "I don't know why you asked me to dine with you. You have no real interest in Annie's progress."

He did care about Annie's welfare, as he would about anyone living under his roof, but he couldn't connect his emotion with action. "I'm trying."

"It's surprising to me that you have such a poor contact with your own daughter. You ought to be proud over her progress."

"I am—thanks to you. At least I now know I'm not housing a dimwit."

Elinor stared at him as if she couldn't believe her ears. "Dimwit? That is the most callous, unfeeling sentiment I've heard voiced from a parent."

They stared at each other for a long tense moment.

"I thought you had changed after all that you told me last night, changed your ways," she said.

"Rome wasn't built in one day."

She looked angry. Pink blossomed in her cheeks, and her eyes flashed dark fire.

"I don't know how to go about making friends with Annie," he said, knowing it was true. The realization made him feel foolish.

"Children are easy to get along with. You listen to them and show them respect, and you'll get it back tenfold."

"Mayhap you can teach me," he said lamely.

"Where were you when she was born?" she asked in a low, angry voice.

"I was at Lyons Court. Phoebe lived here and I lived at the Court. We had very little interaction, especially when she was expecting Annie."

"Oh," she replied, her expression incredulous.

"'Tis the truth. You can ask anyone. Ask Simon. He'll tell you about the state of my marriage."

"If anyone is going to tell me, it's going to be you, my lord. I don't go around and gossip with others."

"For some reason I believe that. You're a very sincere woman, Elinor."

"You don't know who you might hurt while gossiping."

She looked at him as if expecting that he would tell her the story of his marriage, but he found something blocked his throat and that he couldn't get the words out. He swallowed, but the lump was still there. "Someday I'll tell you—that is, if the memories ever get any less painful."

"They do if you stop running away from them. If you can find a way to accept the truth of the situation—"

He lowered his voice, but the force behind his words surprised even him. "'Tis the damned truth that mocks me every day. I'll never accept the situation."

Her eyes grew huge, as if she were on the verge of crying.

"I apologize for my crudeness," he muttered, fighting the urge to push back his chair and march out of the room.

"I believe truth is the least painful when it comes to resolving problems."

"You don't know what you're talking about," he said and found himself engulfed in a wave of anger so vast he had to fight for his breath. He didn't know what to do with the emotion. Helpless, he closed his eyes and followed his own tortured breath as it brought that life-saving air into his lungs. He abhorred the feeling of weakness and hated the burning sensation behind his eyelids.

When she placed a comforting hand on his arm, he fought his first impulse to throw her off. "I don't need your sympathy," he said between clenched teeth.

She pulled away. "I'm sorry."

"Don't apologize! You don't have anything to be sorry about."

She didn't respond, and he could've kicked himself. "I think this conversation has derailed, and it would be advantageous to remove myself from your presence."

"You invited me to share your meal, yet you're going to leave me in front of the servants and set the gossip flying?"

Her eyes blazed with anger as he looked at her, and that stabbed him as much as any misdeed Phoebe had presented him with. He knew Elinor was nothing like Phoebe and he needed to apologize, but no words came. They would've fallen flat anyway. He felt no forgiveness in his frozen heart.

He raised his voice so the servants could hear him. "I'm glad to find out Annie is doing so well in the schoolroom." Every word was a major effort, and he wished he'd never invited Elinor to share his meal.

"I'm impressed with Lady Annabelle's abilities," she replied mechanically. She refused to look at him as she finished the last of the soup. Folding her hands in her lap, she stared out the window.

He pushed away his plate, his bread unfinished. Every minute that passed, a chasm widened between them, and he didn't know how to bring back the feeling of camaraderie he'd felt last night.

"I'd better return to the children, if you'll permit it, my lord," she said without any note of subservience. He knew she was angry with him. Not that he'd wanted any show of humility from her.

"Yes . . . it has been a pleasure, Mrs. Browning," he said and rose as she did.

With a stiff nod, she left the room. Her dark blue skirts swished against a chair as she hurried to get away from him. He stared at her straight back that showed her attitude of no compromise.

Again that sensation of helplessness came over him. There was no way to truly understand females.

He threw down his napkin and left the chamber. That spurt of anger had drained him, and he sought to alleviate the state of desolation slowly engulfing him. Work would help. The familiarity of everyday activity kept him sane.

And he would stay away from Elinor. Any interaction with her touched him too close to his emotions. He was sure she would welcome his distance.

He would've been surprised to discover she shared his helplessness. She'd never encountered a situation like this. She sincerely wanted to help the earl overcome his pain, but where would she start?

She told herself she was doing it for Annie, but to be truthful, she wanted to get closer to him. The realization frightened her. *If you think you have a future with the Ice King, you're building sand castles,* she told herself. Just for one paltry kiss in the dark. Besides, the man was emotionally flawed.

The earl would never consider her more than Annie's governess. If she thought anything other than that, she was an utter fool, she berated herself. A fool she'd never been, and wouldn't start now. Romantic dreams were for starstruck young girls recently out of the schoolroom, not for matrons once widowed. Who was she to believe she could change the earl? If he chose to be bitter and angry, there was nothing she could do about it.

She would forget about the man and his difficulties and concentrate solely on the children. They were her single responsibility.

She took a deep breath that locked away any hopes for romance and stepped into the schoolroom, where a shower of giggles met her.

Eight

The next few days Elinor did everything to avoid the earl, and he evidently had the same idea. She crossed paths with him only once, and all he gave her was a cold, "Good morning, Mrs. Browning."

So it was back to "Mrs. Browning" now.

After the midday meal of fish and potato pie, she decided to take the children for a walk. Before she could act, she heard a wild commotion downstairs in the foyer. She went to look down the curving staircase, and found to her utter surprise that her sister Evelyn had arrived with three of her five children. Simon was in the process of ushering them inside as the butler looked on in consternation.

The children chased each other around the round Chinese table, and Elinor feared for the priceless vase on top filled with flowers. Her sister's lame admonitions were drowned in the melee.

She ran down the stairs in a flurry of skirts and gripped her spirited nephews by their arms as they careened by her. "Henry, Alfred! If you don't calm down this instant, I'll throw you outside in the snow."

They looked up at her gleefully, and as they recognized who she was, they embraced her legs in happiness. She couldn't keep up her anger.

"There you are, my dear," Simon cried out as he caught a glimpse of her.

"What are you doing here?" she asked her sister. "I'm employed as a governess, and you come through the front door as if—"

"I was taking Evelyn home, and we had a small mishap with the carriage near here," Simon explained. "I couldn't very well leave her and the children to suffer in the cold while another coach was arranged." He kissed Elinor's hand. "You look lovely as ever."

Elinor blushed. "Thank you, Simon. You look quite handsome. Is that a new coat I spy?"

"Stultz himself tailored it for me," Simon explained with pride.

Evelyn looked around the vast foyer with awe as she swung baby Rosalyn in her arms. "I had no idea of the grandeur, Elinor. You work in a veritable castle."

"A tomb is more like it," Elinor replied drily.

She hadn't noticed the earl approach until she heard him at her shoulder. Too late did she realize he must've overheard her.

"I'm sorry to hear the mansion gives you morbid thoughts," he said sotto voce. He shook hands with Simon and asked to be introduced to Evelyn. His eyebrows rose as he realized the family connection. "Mrs. Browning spoke of you and her nieces and nephews kindly." He threw a withering glance at the boys, who were now rolling around the floor.

Mortified, Elinor hastened to gather the rambunctious pair and led them upstairs where they could play with Alex and Annie. When she came back downstairs, she discovered Simon had invited himself and Evelyn for a cup of tea. As she reached the foyer, the earl was giving clipped orders to Winslow, who looked less than excited, and Simon was ushering Evelyn and the baby into the parlor that had been decorated in mostly blue and silver.

She reached the earl just as Winslow left the foyer. "I'm sorry about the intrusion, my lord. I had no idea Simon would even think of bringing my sister here."

He didn't look angry. "Simon is family. He comes and goes as he wants here. He paused as if reminded by some memory. "I can't deny you your family. I miss my sister. This is the perfect opportunity for you to spend some time with yours."

Elinor didn't know how to respond. It was true, of course, but the thought of her sister overstepping the bounds of propriety bothered her. She knew, however, how persuasive Simon could be. Evelyn hadn't appeared to care about protocol. She'd obviously been in a total daze.

Even as she fought the feeling, Elinor felt flustered. She joined Simon and Evelyn and discovered the earl had stepped through the door behind her. That added to her discomfort. What if someone said something to raise his ire? Then she berated herself for her unreasonable fear. She wasn't responsible for her sister's or Simon's behavior.

"'Tis a perishing day outside," Evelyn said. "I hope

I can get back home before another storm brews. We've had an uncommon wintry season in Kent. I've never seen so much snow before Christmas!"

"'Tis a time for roasted chestnuts and port in front of the fire," Simon said, his backside turned to the meager fire in fireplace behind him.

"I can't oblige, old fellow," said the earl. "I haven't seen hide nor hair of chestnuts so far this season."

"Mayhap you have to order them," Simon said. "I could do with a glass of port, though."

The earl gestured to the footman by the door, who went to fulfill Simon's wish.

"Nothing like port to warm your insides," Simon said, rubbing his hands. He smiled at Elinor. "You look more beautiful every day, my dear."

Elinor squirmed under the compliment as she sat next to her sister on a low settee. She noticed a cloud pass across the earl's face. Perhaps he thought she had her cap set on Simon, who would be a good catch for someone in her circumstances. "Thank you Simon, but you know your compliments are falling on deaf ears."

"'Tis clear to me you heard it," he said with a chuckle.

"You don't lack in self-confidence, which is a good thing, no doubt," Elinor replied with a smile. *The gall of the man.*

"I wrote to you right before I made this trip to London, dear sister," Evelyn said, and gently lowered the sleeping baby to her lap. "Kind Florence wanted to see the children for the day, and I realized there wouldn't been enough time to see you as well, but look at this fortunate coincidence—here we are!"

"I doubt I would've been able to see you anyway, as my duties here take up most of my time," Elinor said. "How's Florence?"

"As nos—inquisitive and vigorous as ever. She claims her drink of raw eggs mixed with a herbal concoction every morning keeps her eternally young."

"There might be some truth to it. She's seventy if she's a day," Simon said. "I should get the recipe."

"You could never put raw eggs past my lips first thing in the morning," the earl said.

Elinor agreed with him on that. "Florence is somewhat eccentric," she said.

"I know all about it, as she's my aunt—one of the more eccentric ones," the earl said drily.

"She dotes on all of us, especially Evelyn," Elinor said with a fond look at her sister. Who could find fault with Evelyn's kind face and gentle ways?

They shared the same coloring, but Elinor stood several inches taller. However much she searched inside, Elinor didn't think she could find the depth of sweetness that Evelyn had. Everyone, including old people, animals, and children, flocked around Evelyn to enjoy her company.

"She loves the children and complains her grandchildren are away," Evelyn said simply. "You have only one, Elinor. Not enough in Florence's eye."

"You're probably right on that score, and I think I'll continue to disappoint her in that area."

"Don't say that," Evelyn said with her bell-like

laugh. "Fate has a way of working magic when you least expect it. Mayhap there will be a special blessing for you at Christmas that will change your life."

"I have an invitation to a Christmas dance at Lady Stanton's," Simon interrupted. "She's quite a wonderful old lady. Would you like to come with me, Elinor? You need to get away from the children at times and just enjoy yourself."

"That's very kind of you, Simon, but—"

"Don't be silly, Elinor," her sister interrupted. "You can't deny Simon the pleasure of your company. Besides, you can use the break in your routine."

Elinor looked uncertainly at the earl, wondering if he would find it acceptable that someone in his employ would hobnob with the gentry. Not that she didn't have the right background, but things were different now, and she had to live by the new rules.

"*I* invited you," Simon said. "Don't look to Lucas for permission."

The earl directed his dark brown gaze at her, and she had the overwhelming sensation he could see right through her. For a moment the whole room and everyone in it faded away. She could see only the intensity of his eyes, and it perturbed her that he had any kind of power over her feelings.

Heat rose in her face, and she moved uncomfortably in her seat. "I'm flattered, Simon, but—"

"Don't turn down an invitation on my account," the earl said noncommittally. "What you do in your spare time is none of my business."

"Amen!" Simon exclaimed. "Say you accept my invitation."

"Yes, I would enjoy that very much," she said, and meant it. Work without play could be very wearisome.

"You need to kindle the Christmas spirit," Simon said.

"Isn't it a bit early for that?" the earl commented sourly.

"'Tis never too early for holiday cheer," Simon countered. "I shall enjoy seeing you in a fine gown rather than the homespun if bright garb you wear these days, dear Elinor. Something red with a nice shine to it."

She laughed. "You're incorrigible, Simon. I have no reason to purchase anything red in my current position. Besides, I don't look good in red; it clashes with the color of my hair." She felt uncomfortable discussing such intimate details with a gentleman.

"You have impeccable taste," Simon said.

She noticed a thundercloud had descended on the earl's brow, and she wondered if they'd gone too far.

"Desist, Simon. You're talking without thinking." Elinor turned to her sister and admired the sleeping baby.

"We're all family," Simon continued. "There's nothing to be embarrassed about."

The earl spoke up. "You're embarrassing the ladies. I realize you would say anything to me—you never had a problem with that," he said ruefully, "but 'tis the first time I meet Mrs. Browning's sister, mind you."

"It's about time you get better acquainted. I think you'll see a lot more of Elinor's family."

"I will?" the earl commented, his voice incredulous.

"Certainly not!" Elinor said hurriedly. "No one shall darken your doorstep without your consent."

"Don't be silly," Simon said. "This place sadly needs cheering up, and who better to do it than a gaggle of children?" He turned to the earl. "Don't you agree?"

The earl stared gloomily at the window. "You leave me no choice—"

"No need even to respond," Elinor said, now mortified. "My nieces and nephews won't bother you. I can promise you that." She addressed Simon, now angry. "You'll have to respect my wishes on this."

As she finished speaking, the door flew open and four whirlwinds swept into the room, Annie leading the way. High-pitched voices and laughter rose to the ceiling.

"I'll catch you now, Annie," Albert roared, and Alex yelled at the top of his lungs, "Hide under the table, Annie!"

The girl giggled and began rolling under the fringed tablecloth when the earl gripped her legs and halted her progress. The boys careened into him, and all noise died abruptly. They stood in awe, four pairs of eyes staring up at his stern face.

"Lord Lyons," Alex said. "We didn't know you were in here, or we wouldn't—"

"Shh, Alex," Elinor admonished. She grabbed

their arms and pushed them unceremoniously toward the door. The last half hour had been a nightmare. She watched as the earl hauled Annie to her feet. Annie started crying and rushed to Elinor's side.

"Please excuse me. I'll have to take the children back to the schoolroom." She ushered the miscreants out of the room. "Where are your manners, children? You know you're not allowed down here without an adult guiding you. Where's Nanny?"

"She fell asleep, Mrs. Browning," Annie explained. "She was very tired today."

They found Nanny Wendell sitting in a rocking chair, her head lolling on her chest. Elinor shook her shoulder, and she awakened with a start. "What?"

"You let the children run wild," Elinor said.

The nanny apologized, and Elinor left the rambunctious group with her, then went to her room to calm herself down.

She splashed ice cold water on her face from the bowl on her wash stand, and patted herself dry. Why did Simon insist on complimenting her in front of the earl? To him it might not be an important matter, but it was to her. She took some deep breaths to calm herself. She dipped her fingertips in rose water and dabbed it on her throat, then rearranged her hair—even if it didn't need it.

After spending time calming down, she went back downstairs only to discover that her sister and Simon had left. The butler approached her.

"Mr. Nelson apologizes, but the replacement

coach arrived, and the infant started fretting. They send their greetings, and your sister asked me to tell you she'll write."

"Thank you, Winslow."

She sought the Ice King in the library, finding him alone. "I don't want to take any of your time, but I have to apologize for the lapse in my duties."

He set down the book in his hand and leaned his elbows on his desk. If he was going to berate her, she feared she might explode. She'd been holding her emotions tightly wound all day.

He looked at her for a long moment. "Part of me desires to rake you over the coals, but another part of me wants to explore what we started last night. I don't see how I can chastise you and hope to get sympathy and warmth in return."

"Sympathy and warmth?" she echoed, confused.

"Last night you gave me a great deal of support, Elinor, and even though I have a tendency to be ruthless, I can't help but remember those tender moments."

"I doubted you'd remember. 'Twas one of those meetings that are unexpected and, once over, rapidly forgotten."

"You don't know me very well."

She shook her head. "That's natural, seeing as I've only known you for a few weeks."

"Less than that. We've never talked as we did last night."

I saw you as an ogre and a dimwit, she thought, remembering how she'd despised his remoteness, especially toward his daughter.

"One night doesn't constitute a friendship."

He rose, disappointment fighting with determination in his expression. "No, it doesn't, but I shared things with you that I've never told a soul." He walked around the desk and stood in front of her.

"And I will keep the confidence." She felt that familiar heat rising to her face again, and she wondered why her life seemed to be going out of control. He stood so close she could smell the sandalwood soap he used. Fighting the urge to step back, she faced him squarely.

He put his hands on her shoulders and pulled her close. She couldn't find an ounce of strength to fight him.

"I don't know . . . but I have to do this," he murmured. He leaned over her and kissed her, his tongue intimate and insistent in her mouth, taking her breath away. She had never felt anything so close and intimate, not even with Matthew, whose kisses she had enjoyed. This was like plunging into the depths of someone's soul and drowning in the blissful feeling.

But it was all wrong, wasn't it? her mind cried as he plundered her.

Taking a deep breath, she tried to tear away, but he held her so tightly she couldn't move. Panicking, she struggled, and he loosened his grip.

His breath came in rapid bursts against her cheek. He gently pushed her away, and she leaned against the back of a tall wing chair, catching her own breath.

"I don't know why you chose to do that," she said

in a low, trembling voice. "Let me inform you, I'll never be your lightskirt. You may be a man who trifles with the servants, but you cannot trifle with me."

"The thought never entered my mind, and I've never been interested in trifling with any of my staff. If I wanted someone for an evening, there are plenty of companions to choose from on the town."

She lowered her gaze, worried that she'd overreacted. "Then why, if I may ask, did you kiss me?"

He remained silent for a long moment. "Truly, I don't know. If I could explain it to myself, I would explain it to you."

His reply frustrated her. "Life can't be that complicated. It isn't to me."

"Nothing is simple to me at this time. My life has been turned upside down because of the appearance of the ghosts."

"I'd say that would shake anyone up," she said. "Serves you right."

"You're cruel," he said, but his lips turned up at the corners.

"I can be when it's needed."

"I have no fear you would hesitate to call me on the carpet, and look at how you've taken over my house! You fill the mansion with unruly children and permanently increasing women and let my cousin ride roughshod over me at all hours."

"I'm sure you can handle Simon without much strain, but that you would accuse me of something he did is unfair. My sister isn't constantly in the family way, and no one came to personally disturb you. In fact, you chose to be there."

"Appears she is increasing to me," he said, and looked heavenward as if some mysterious power there could protect him from more invasions of such persons in the future.

"She may be, but that's no business of yours."

"Thank heaven for that!"

"Now you're being impossible, my lord."

"Just practical. The poor gentleman who has to feed them has no peace at all, unless he's rich as Croesus."

"Mayhap he is, and mayhap he's a close friend to the Prince Regent."

"Then I would know him, and I don't."

"More's the pity. Robert is a good man, a humble clergyman. Someone to have on your side."

"No doubt he'd be ready to barge in here unbidden with all the others if he had the opportunity."

"You're being unreasonable, Lord Lyons." Instead of appreciating his dry humor, she felt annoyed. She straightened her back and made sure all stray locks of hair were tucked under her lace cap. "I refuse to listen to any more insults about my family. When you're willing to acknowledge yours—Annie—we might have another discussion. Good afternoon."

She left the room wishing she'd never laid eyes on the Earl of Lyons.

Nine

The night of the Christmas dance at Lady Stanton's came, and Simon arrived at the appointed hour to pick up Elinor. She wore a simple rose empire-style gown with matching roses tucked into her hair and a strand of pearls around her neck, jewelry Matthew had given her the last Christmas they were together.

She wore them tonight to remind herself that in her heart she was still married to him, and to keep her safe from the possibility someone in Simon's circle might find her interesting.

If she had to explain to someone about her employment, she wouldn't be able to face the expression of horror that would appear without fail. Part of her regretted going. Another part of her longed terribly to get out and enjoy herself. She doubted anyone would enquire, but someone might know about her circumstances and gossip. Hopefully, everyone she knew had retired to their country estates for the Christmas season. Only a few of the gentry stayed in London.

Simon greeted her in the hallway. "You look lovely, Elinor."

He helped her with her long wool cape, and she'd already pulled on her gloves. He gave her a nosegay of carnations and rosebuds, which he helped her fasten to her wrist.

"Thank you, Simon. You're so kind."

He kissed her enthusiastically on the cheek just as the earl stepped down the stairs dressed in a coat, beaver hat, and sturdy gloves. His neckcloth lay in expertly tied white folds, and she could see the lapels of an immaculate evening coat. Evidently he had his own plans for the night.

His gaze raked over her, from her newly washed and curled hair to the tips of her slippers, dyed the same rose color as her dress. She longed for him to say she looked beautiful, but he looked angry.

No compliments came over the lips that had kissed her so passionately not long ago. She could almost feel the imprint of them now.

"Looks as if you changed your mind, old fellow. Are you coming with us?" Simon asked heartily.

The earl shook his head. "No, I'm dining at the club tonight."

"Should be a boring evening, then. You can always drop by later, seeing as you must've gotten an invitation."

"Yes, but—" He let the words drop. "A good table and a bottle of wine are what tempt me tonight."

"We are going to dance, aren't we, Elinor?" Simon took her arm possessively. "You'll be very popular, and I consider myself very fortunate."

"I look forward to it," she said, and meant it. "It has been a long time since I danced."

She shot a glance at her employer and noticed his closed expression, but his eyes were alive with a strange fire, as if he was struggling to keep himself from exploding. Why would he be angry? she asked herself. Certainly they hadn't done anything to stir his anger.

"Let's go, my dear. The magical coach is waiting."

She smiled and placed her begloved hand in Simon's. For once she felt elegant and admired.

A blustery wind flew across the pavement and tore at her cloak, but the icy cold had let up some, and a foggy drizzle came down to touch her skin with dew. She was grateful for the cover of the coach.

"I pray the wheel was repaired correctly," Simon said as he joined her inside. "I've had recurring problems with it. I might need a new one."

He treated her with great courtesy during the evening, and the kind hostess didn't seem to care about her background. The dance had an informal air, and Elinor enjoyed herself. It had been too long since she had gone to any kind of entertainment. Life was drab without it.

The ballroom had been decorated with holly and baskets of grapes and oranges that sent out a sweet fragrance.

Delicacies like mince pies, plum puddings, iced cakes, and bonbons of all shapes tempted the guests beside the huge bowl of wassail, from which Elinor had several servings. The drink went to her head immediately, making her giddy.

After dancing with several gentlemen and finishing a waltz with Simon, she cooled herself with her fan as he fetched her another glass of wassail. *Water would be more appropriate,* she thought.

Candlelight glowed golden, elegant people in shimmering silks and satins chatted and laughed around her, and she enjoyed the music of the violinists in the corner. What a stroke of luck Simon had asked her to join him. A fleeting thought of the earl brushed through her, and she felt a pinch in her heart as if missing him.

Balderdash! she thought. He wasn't someone she would miss, nor would he miss her. Whatever had transpired between them meant very little; just moments of weakness, really.

Still, her heartbeat increased as she remembered their kisses, and she wondered if he'd felt the same power behind them.

It shamed her to admit even to herself that she'd never experienced anything that moving with Matthew.

Matthew had been good and solid, not unpredictable and dangerous. Yes, she thought, the earl was dangerous; he affected her more than she would've liked. She had to remember he wasn't a *man,* he was her employer and Annie's father.

Simon returned, interrupting her reverie. "You looked as if you were lost in the stars, my dear."

She accepted the glass from his hand. "Thank you, Simon."

"I take it you don't want to share your thoughts."

She shook her head. "Nothing to share. Just silly musings."

"I hope they weren't about me if they were silly," he said with a laugh.

She smiled. "No, not at all."

"Speaking of silly, Lucas was—for not joining us here at this bright gathering." He clasped his hands on his back and rolled on the balls of his feet. "However, I must say he appears a bit lighter. He even tried a small joke the other day. I would rejoice to see the old Lucas return to us."

"'Tis hard for me to believe he has a lighter side, and I'm sorry to say that about my employer."

"Don't worry about formalities. I know you respect him—as he respects you. I sense without having heard it from his own lips that he's suprised at your dedication to your work."

"I like working with Annie. She is a spark of light in that house. She's adorable, to be sure, and very inquisitive."

"It has been my mother's heartbreak to watch Lucas, her nephew, wither away in that mansion. He used to be friendly and open to all sorts of larks after he came down to London as a young buck. Once he got free of the parental yoke, he blossomed. He came to embrace life as if it had been something held back from him before."

"Would you say he was popular with the young ladies?" she asked and sipped her wassail.

"Yes, very. He, however, didn't seem to take anything seriously. He flirted and danced, courted and enjoyed, mostly to the consternation of the matchmaking mamas who had their avid eyes on his immense fortune. No one could nab him until he met Phoebe, and his life would've been a lot easier if they'd never met."

Her curiosity awakened, she longed to hear more, but she noticed Simon wore an uneasy expression. She didn't push for more information.

"Annie looks a lot like her mother," he said, as if to conclude the conversation on a sure note.

"I'd say she has to. She doesn't have the Lyons' dark eyes or hair."

He glanced at the ceiling and chewed on his full bottom lip as if in the throes of a dilemma. She could see him battling with himself. "There are a few things you don't know, my dear, but I fear Lucas would be incensed if I divulged them. Deep, dark family secrets," he said sotto voce. "Not that they are that secret, mind you, but 'tis not my place to speak about them."

"I appreciate your discretion," she said, and she did. Simon was not and never would be a gossip.

"My point is that I think Lucas is improving. I saw a spark in his eye I haven't seen for years, and that, my dear, is heartening." He patted her shoulder. "And all thanks to you. I believe you're bringing about a miracle. I don't know how, but things have changed since you moved in."

"You're kind, Simon." She couldn't remember an evening this pleasant since Matthew died, but she feared Simon would become enamored with her, and that wouldn't do. She could not think of him in any other manner than a sweet-tempered brother. "We'd better leave before—"

"My dear, don't worry about the children," he interrupted. "The nanny is quite capable of taking care of them."

"You're right, but I'm afraid all this dancing has made me quite fatigued, and the wassail has inebriated me."

"Come now, my fair, I don't believe that for a moment. You're a lively dancer." As if to prove his point, he pulled her back into a set of country dances, and she couldn't help but laugh.

When they'd finished their dance, she glanced toward the gilded door of the ballroom and was startled to see Lucas standing there, his eyes directed at her. His gaze burned into her, leaving her quite breathless.

"He did join us after all," Simon said as he saw his cousin. "That's excellent. I believe this is the first time he's accepted an invitation since Phoebe died."

They walked over to him. "Lucas, old fellow, I'm pleased." Simon slapped him on the shoulder. "Must be lonely to always dine alone."

"That's not the point," Lucas said cautiously. He looked at Elinor as if to measure her state of mind. "It has been a long time since I saw Lady Stanton, and she's one of my friends."

Simon nodded. "I'm sure she was as surprised to see you as I was."

Lucas said, "She certainly was, but that's neither here nor there."

"Why don't you dance with Elinor?" Simon asked. "I'm here to make sure she's enjoying herself."

Elinor fluttered her fan across her heated face. "I

daresay I'm too tired for another dance right now, but thank you for your thoughtfulness." She couldn't see herself in the arms of the earl, floating around the floor in a waltz, not while he was her employer. She couldn't believe Simon would suggest such a thing, but then he saw her as the "old" Elinor. She wasn't sure how the earl saw her, not after the kisses they'd shared. Boggy terrain indeed.

Feeling uncomfortable, she shivered as if a cold draft had drifted over her. The earl didn't look at ease as he glanced away from her and then back.

"I'm going to have a chat with the hostess before we leave," Simon said, and hurried across the room to catch up with Lady Stanton.

Elinor wished he hadn't left her alone with the earl.

They stared at each other, trying to find something to converse about.

"She decorated beautifully, don't you agree?" Elinor said lamely, pointing at the holly.

"Certainly." He wore a bored expression.

New arrivals, a group of gentlemen, entered, laughing heartily. Elinor didn't recognize anyone. None had belonged to her former circle. The earl tensed beside her, and she followed his gaze to a tall gentleman with blond hair and clear blue eyes.

"Who's that, a friend of yours?"

"No . . . not exactly," he growled. He looked pale, as if a sudden illness had struck him. "It's Lord Swindon."

"Oh," she said, waiting for him to expound, but he didn't.

"Excuse me, Elinor, but I have to leave." He gave her a curt bow and headed toward the door. When he passed the gentlemen, Lord Swindon called out his name in a overly cordial voice, and tension rose in the room, which puzzled her. All eyes had turned to them.

She couldn't hear the words they exchanged, but she could see they were harsh. Within seconds, the earl had left, his back stiff with anger.

Simon returned. "Lucas didn't stay very long, did he?"

"No, about ten minutes. Simon, who is Lord Swindon?"

"Someone Lucas doesn't get along with. I saw him leave in a rage. There were great problems with Lord Swindon and Phoebe."

Elinor read between the lines and knew the animosity had been long standing.

"One day he'll tell you about it, I'm sure," Simon stated, thus informing her he wasn't the one to divulge Lucas's past.

"The tension was strong enough for the earl to have called out Lord Swindon," she commented.

"Yes . . . yes. As a matter of fact, he already did. Several years ago."

"Evidently neither one of them was killed."

"Swindon was laid up for months nursing a stomach wound. Lucas almost had to leave the country to protect himself from being prosecuted, but luckily he had powerful friends in the right places. The scandal fizzled out for the lack of fuel."

Elinor desired to know more, but Simon

changed the subject and Lord Swindon moved out of her vision. She was getting tired; it had been a long day.

The clock in St. Mark's church chimed eleven as they donned their cloaks and spoke for their carriage.

"I'm disappointed," Simon said. "'Tis only eleven and you insist on returning home."

"It has been a splendid evening, Simon. I've had enough exertion for a sixmonth, and drunk enough wassail to drown."

He laughed and led her outside, where the drizzle had turned to icy rain. Icicles hung delicately from the wet black branches, and the walk to the carriage appeared quite treacherous, but they managed without slipping and falling.

"I say, the weather has turned. We'll see more snow by the morrow," Simon said and looked toward the sky as if seeking some answer from the blackness.

"You're probably right. 'Tis much colder than when we left."

They traveled in silence. The drive seemed to take forever due to the slow pace to spare the horses any injury. The coach felt wobbly, as if favoring one side. Finally, Simon called through the hatch for the driver to halt their progress.

"What's wrong?" Elinor asked.

"The front right side of the coach is unsteady—something about the wheel, no doubt. It's the same one that failed when I took your sister home, and it looks as if the wheelwright didn't make solid repairs." He got out of the carriage, and she heard the muffled conversation with the driver. The horses stomped and snorted.

Simon returned inside. "I'm afraid the wheel is about to come off. The nave now has a large crack. It's unfortunate, and I'll have a sharp word with the wheelwright tomorrow." He took one of her hands in his. "Not to worry. I'm going to send one of the lackeys to Grosvenor Square. We're not far from there."

"Don't concern yourself about me. I'm grateful you caught the problem before we had an accident." She placed her feet on the heated brick on the floor and snuggled under the blanket he had tucked around her at the outset.

He went outside to talk to the footmen at the back of the coach, and within the minute he had returned inside. "It's growing more chilly by the hour," he said and rubbed his hands together to keep warm. "My man will be back shortly with Lucas's carriage."

He had barely said the words before a familiar coach stopped beside them. The only lights were the lanterns at each side of the driver's seat, and they stared through the window at the vehicle.

"By God, it's Lucas! That was quick." Simon jumped down and found Lucas himself occupied the coach.

She overheard them talk, and Simon returned, the Ice King in tow. "Most fortunate. Lucas is accomplishing an errand before putting away the coach for the night. He recognized my rig." He held out his hand toward her. "Elinor, you might as well go with him. I have to deal with this problem now. Can't very well leave the horseflesh to freeze to death."

Lucas appeared at his side and glanced at Elinor.

"As I said, Simon, you can bring the equipage to Grosvenor Square and deal with the problem tomorrow," Lucas reiterated.

"I'd rather take the horses home, if you don't mind."

"Suit yourself."

Simon reached out for Elinor. She complied, and Simon helped her down and escorted her to the earl's carriage. It felt warm inside and smelled like the earl, masculine and powerful. Simon said goodbye, and Lucas stepped inside. The door closed behind them, and they were alone in the coach.

She could barely see him in the dark, only feel his gaze upon her. The equipage moved along the street.

"Did you enjoy the evening?" he asked.

"Very much, thank you."

"Simon is an attentive suitor."

Did she detect a hint of tension in his voice? She wasn't certain, but surely it wasn't important.

"Are we going directly home?" she asked.

"We're going to deliver my secretary's food basket that he forgot earlier. Cook sends victuals with him sometimes, as he has fifteen mouths to feed."

"Heavens, fifteen! I don't know how they survive."

"It's not easy. Brinkley is a hardworking and honest fellow. You'd never hear him complain about anything. Every day is beautiful to him."

"Hmm, seems he would rub you the wrong way," she said, unable to keep the comment from rushing forth.

"Just as the words left my mouth, I knew as surely as the sun rises that you would find a sarcastic comment in return, Elinor."

"I apologize."

"Why? I know you don't feel repentant in your heart," he said, sounding put upon.

"You cannot tell me what's in my heart and what isn't, my lord."

"In this instance I could, and don't make me regret offering my assistance."

"I wouldn't dream of it," she said.

"But your voice holds a teasing note."

"I can't help that. I'm convinced the wassail had a lot more than cider." She glanced out the window into the pitch blackness. "Where does Mr. Brinkley live?"

"I offered him a cottage at Lyons Court, but his wife prefers the metropolis where she was born. They live near Haymarket."

The coach rattled over the cobbled streets, and Elinor wondered if they would reach their destination in this weather. "'Tis a difficult night to travel," she said.

"We're not going far. I never thought you would be fearful. You appear a fearless lioness."

"I suppose that is a compliment—and coming from you, it's a great one."

Silence hung between them as they both mulled over what she'd said.

"I . . ." she began, knowing she'd insulted him.

"Don't bother. The least said . . ." He paused. "You're right, you know. I don't give out compliments easily."

She blushed and was grateful he couldn't notice her embarrassment in the dark. "Furthermore, I doubt I'm a lioness. I'm surprised you would see me that way."

"How would you describe yourself then?"

She thought for a moment. "I have a lot of fortitude, something I've learned over the years."

"And courage."

She heard the sincerity in his voice and wished she could see his expression. "Thank you."

"It takes a lot of bravery to move into the world and create a life for yourself and your child."

She pondered his words for a moment. "'Twas the only thing to do. I refuse to live on charity while I'm capable of employment."

He sighed deeply, as if disturbed by her statement, but didn't reply. "We'll be at Brinkley's house shortly."

They didn't speak during the rest of the trip, and wind battered the coach. Shortly, the horses came to a halt, and she could see oil lamps swinging from poles along the road, few and far between. Snow lay in drifts along the walls and swagged the bottom of every windowpane.

The cold crept through every crevice and slid along the floor, but as the earl stepped outside, she saw the bright candlelight in the windows where the Brinkleys lived, and it cheered her.

"I would like to meet Mrs. Brinkley," she said. Not waiting for his consent, she stepped outside, her feet already frozen in her thin slippers.

The footmen at the back brought around a large basket and knocked on the door. Within seconds, a child in a nightshirt and slippers opened it and called out. "'Tis the earl, Papa!"

Brinkley appeared, his eyes round with surprise behind his spectacles. "My lord! Mrs. Browning, I've never!" He gestured them forward. "Don't stand there in the cold. Come in, come in." He called into the house. "Helen, we have guests. Bring out some food."

The earl and Elinor moved further into the house. The scent of roasted meat and onions filled the air, and the rooms were filled with warmth, even though the fire in the grate struggled to keep going.

"We dined early, but there should be plenty left," Mr. Brinkley said.

"Please, don't concern yourself with that. We've dined," the earl said firmly.

Children ran around the room, creating an overpowering din. They clung to Mr. Brinkley, and when Helen appeared, they ran in circles around her. She admonished them with good humor. Beaming a smile at the earl and Elinor, she stepped forward and curtsied. "My lord, I'm bowled over with surprise that you've come to our humble abode."

Elinor noticed the worn brown fabric of her gown and the places that had been carefully mended. The only color blazoned in her cheeks and in the red ribbons on her sleeves and along the hem of her skirt. Rotund and comfortable, she looked happy, and her children did, too.

Mr. Brinkley introduced Elinor to her, and Helen took both of Elinor's hands between hers. "I hear such good things about you, Mrs. Browning. You're working a miracle with little Annie, and I can see why. 'Tis clear to me you have that warmth children like."

"Why, thank you, Mrs. Brinkley." She glanced at the many children around them, who looked up with bright faces. "You must have a soft spot for the little ones."

"Oh, yes!" She spread her arms. "This is some of my brood." She looked around as if searching for someone. "Where is Jimmy?" She explained to Elinor. "He's one of my younger ones, only five, and he's not strong."

From the kitchen beyond came a small child leaning on a crutch. His leg was twisted, and his face looked pale and drawn as if there never was enough to eat, but nevertheless there was a happy light in his eyes. "Papa, look at the basket. I know't Mrs. Braithewaite put some apples in, and I pray Cook sent one of her cakes."

Mrs. Brinkley laughed. "That's my Jimmy, always curious about the baskets." She turned to the earl. "I'm ever so grateful to you for your generosity."

The earl shrugged. "Cook is the one to thank. I've got naught to do with this, except for tonight."

"Without it, we wouldn't eat every day," Mrs. Brinkley said humbly. "Mr. Brinkley works very hard, but we have many mouths to feed."

Jimmy stumped over to the basket and peered under the crisp towel that covered the food. "Aye, she sent a currant cake—my favorite."

Elinor stared at the children's worn clothes and leaky shoes. They were a brave but ragged lot. She'd always thought of Mr. Brinkley as a solemn man who cared for nothing but work, and now she knew why. His only desire was to provide for this family the best he could.

Jimmy stuck a thin hand into his father's sturdy grip and looked up at the earl. A tear stuck to his pale lashes. "Cook is ever so kind," he said in his reedy voice.

"I'm certain she is," the earl replied.

Everyone, in a chorus of voices, thanked the earl, and he escorted Elinor to the front door. As they stopped in the tiny hallway so that Elinor could put up her hood and pull the cloak tight, she heard Mrs. Brinkley speak before the door closed completely. "Lord Lyons is a miserable man, isn't he? He has so much to be grateful for and walks about with a face so full of sorrow. It must be no easy thing to work for him, Ian, and for less than you deserve."

"I'm contented with the work, my dear. 'Tis all I've ever known."

Elinor slanted a glance at the earl and noted the

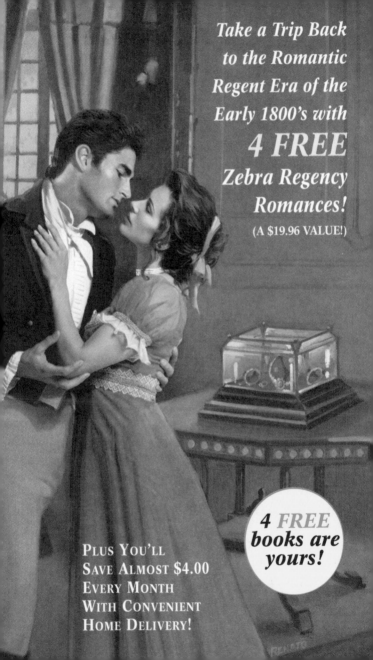

We'd Like to Invite You to Subscribe to Zebra's Regency Romance Book Club and Give You a Gift of 4 Free Books as Your Introduction! (Worth $19.96!)

If you're a Regency lover, imagine the joy of getting 4 FREE Zebra Regency Romances and then the chance to have these lovely stories delivered to your home each month at the lowest price available! Well, that's our offer to you and here' how you benefit by becoming a Regency Romance subscriber:

- **4 FREE** Introductory Regency Romances are delivered to your doorstep (you only pay for shipping and handling)

- 4 BRAND NEW Regencies are then delivered each month (usually before they're available in bookstores)

- Subscribers save almost $4.00 every month

- You also receive a **FREE** monthly newsletter, which features author profiles, discounts, subscriber benefits, book previews and more

- No risks or obligations...in other words, you can cancel whenever you wish with no questions asked

Join the thousands of readers who enjoy the savings and convenience offered to Regency Romance subscribers. After your initial introductory shipment, you receive 4 brand-new Zebra Regency Romances each month to examine for 10 days. Then, if you decide to keep the books, you'll pay the preferred subscriber's price, plus shipping and handling.

It's a no-lose proposition, so return the FREE BOOK CERTIFICATE today!

Say Yes to 4 Free Books!
Complete and return the order card to receive this $19.96 value, ABSOLUTELY FREE!

If the certificate is missing below, write to:
Regency Romance Book Club
P.O. Box 5214, Clifton, New Jersey 07015-5214
or call TOLL-FREE 1-800-770-1963
Visit our website at www.kensingtonbooks.com.

FREE BOOK CERTIFICATE

YES! Please rush me 4 Zebra Regency Romances (I only pay for shipping and handling). I understand that each month thereafter I will be able to preview 4 brand-new Regency Romances FREE for 10 days. Then, if I should decide to keep them, I will pay the money-saving preferred subscriber's price for all 4...that's a savings of 20% off the publisher's price. I may return any shipment within 10 days and owe nothing, and I may cancel this subscription at any time. My 4 FREE books will be mine to keep in any case.

Name _____

Address _____ Apt. ____

City _____ State _____ Zip _____

Telephone ( ) _____

Signature _____ RNHL2A
(If under 18, parent or guardian must sign.)

Terms and prices subject to change. Orders subject to acceptance by Regency Romance Book Club.
Offer valid in U.S. only.

lll..l..l.lll....ll.l.l.l.l.l.l.l.ll.l.l.l..ll.l.l.l

REGENCY ROMANCE BOOK CLUB
Zebra Home Subscription Service, Inc.
P.O. Box 5214
Clifton NJ 07015-5214

PLACE
STAMP
HERE

tightening of his lips. The words must've hurt him, but he pretended he'd heard nothing.

"They are a very happy family. It's quite amazing, isn't it? They have so little, but they are content in each other's company."

"They never have to be lonely," he replied in a neutral voice as if he didn't care.

But she knew he cared. She knew Mrs. Brinkley's words had hurt him deep down, but she had no idea if he would instigate any change. She seriously doubted that he would, and it pained her. When had she started caring for what he did?

Ten

For the next few days the earl sequestered himself in the library, and Elinor didn't see him or talk to him. He'd been unusually quiet on their trip back to Grosvenor Square from the Brinkleys' humble abode, and she'd felt his withdrawal just as keenly as she'd felt the freezing cold of the night.

She had wondered since if anything or anyone would ever manage to pierce his armor. She had not been able, but why would she think she could? Because he'd kissed her twice?

She would have to realize the kisses hadn't mattered to him, but it shocked her to find out they had to her.

He hadn't approached her since that icy night. Why had she thought he would? If she were perfectly honest with herself, she had harbored a secret desire he would approach her with a romantic gesture.

She admonished herself for such thoughts. What did she expect him to say or do? Sweep her into his arms and proclaim eternal love? Hardly.

She spent some time in the kitchen sampling Cook's delicacies with the children. Alex had wrapped everyone around his little finger, and she watched him grow rosy and happy, much more so than when they'd lived alone. He adored Annie, which was an added blessing.

Mrs. Miller, or Cook, who'd been away from the kitchen, came waddling back, her face red with ire. "This is the last straw!" she boomed. "I'm so mad I could spit." She waved a wrinkled piece of paper in her hand as if it had been wadded up and then flattened out again.

"Here's what I'd planned for the Christmas Day feast: geese, brawn, turkey, a suckling pig, sausages, salmon in aspic, mince pies and plum puddings, a mountain of fruit to please the eye with colors, candied ginger, cakes, bonbons and sweets and sugared almonds." She tore off her apron and flung it on a chair.

"What happened?" Elinor asked as chambermaids and kitchen help gathered around the cook with their mouths open.

"The earl took one look at the list and said he wanted nothing special for Christmas. I've never heard the like! Last year was meager, and I could understand that, as he'd lost his wife only a year earlier, but this year—"

Elinor placed a hand on Cook's forearm. "Don't take on so. The earl is not himself, and I daresay he's not planning on spending Christmas Day by himself. Mr. Nelson is sure to invite him to Berkley Street."

"Are we all going to go without at Christmas?" the youngest chambermaid asked timidly.

"I'm sure you're going 'ome to your mother, Mabel," another maid said. "You can't 'xpect anything special from 'is lordship's table."

"He won't deprive you of something out of the ordinary at Christmas," Elinor stated firmly, though she doubted her own words.

They all looked at her as if they didn't believe a word, and she suspected they knew the earl better than she did.

"I shall have a word with him," she said with more determination than she felt inside. She stood, her fists balled at her sides.

"If Christmas Day is just another day here, I shall resign," Cook said, shouting the last word.

Elinor asked the maids to look after the children and headed toward the library. The foyer lay cold and desolate between the domestic regions and the earl's quarters. Before she could lose her courage, she knocked on the library door.

Mr. Brinkley opened it, and smiled at her. "Mrs. Browning, a good morning to you!"

She greeted him kindly. "I'd like a word with his lordship, if he's in."

Mr. Brinkley bowed and enquired of the earl whether he would see her. Evidently he would, as the secretary waved her inside and closed the door behind him as he left them alone.

The earl fastened his dark gaze on her, and she realized instantly he understood why she had come.

"Mrs. Browning, I already gave Cook my decision. Nothing and no one will bend it."

Mrs. Browning, is it? she thought. "You would certainly relent if you could've seen the looks on the servants' faces. Never have I seen such disappointment."

"If you're here to berate me, you've come to the wrong place. I don't care for any kind of feast for Christmas. 'Tis nothing but great excess."

"Or great stinginess on your part. The servants look forward to the festivities all year. You can't deprive them of that." Anger bubbled in her stomach, and she faced the earl across the desk. "And I surmise you would deprive your daughter, as well."

"Annie is too young to know what is going on."

"Not at all! She's well aware of everything, and is looking forward to Christmas, as most children in this city."

He sighed heavily. "I give you carte blanche to create some festivity in the schoolroom. Will that satisfy you?"

"You're trying to fob me off with promises, but I speak for the entire household, not just the children."

"Humbug." He looked mutinous, and she longed to shake some sense into him.

"What happened to the challenge of the apparition? Have you already forgotten your vow to change your life?"

He looked away, but she sensed the pain he felt.

"Not too long ago you called me a fearless lioness. Where did you lose your own courage? I don't know what happened, but you're different since that gathering to which Simon invited me. All I know is you exchanged a few words with Lord

Swindon and decided life had turned back on its track to misery."

"That's nonsense," he said, but he didn't sound very convincing.

"I've never met—"

He stood so quickly the large chair threatened to topple. "Enough's enough! You shall have your feast in the servants' quarters. Tell Cook I—"

The door flew open, interrupting his outburst, and Mrs. Florence Nelson stepped forth, sweeping her arms wide in a great entrance. "Lucas, my dearest nephew, are you suffering a bout of bad temper?" She lifted her jeweled eyeglass and stared at him with a magnified eye.

"Aunt Flo," he said between gritted teeth. "You've chosen the perfect moment to barge in."

"What kind of welcome is that?" she asked haughtily.

Simon entered behind her, his usual beaming self.

"Florence, you have rescued me," Elinor said with a laugh, and kissed the older woman's cheeks. She looked at the elegant fur-trimmed cloak of royal blue velvet with matching hat and ostrich feather dyed dark blue bobbing over one eye. Florence smelled of perfume and powder, her cheeks rouged lightly. With her flair for drama, Mrs. Nelson should've tread the boards, but she'd chosen to follow her heart and marry the man who had loved her with total devotion for most of his life, and still did.

Elinor wondered if she would ever taste a love that would last a lifetime.

"I'm willing to rescue you anytime from this curmudgeon," Simon's mother said with a haughty nod at Lucas.

Elinor threw an uneasy glance at the earl, who stared at his aunt with a hint of reluctant amusement.

"Perhaps you could take her off my hands," the earl drawled. "It would save me a lot of conflict."

"Conflict?" the older woman asked, raising her coal black eyebrows. "Elinor is not a mischief-maker, Lucas—never was."

His gaze raked over Elinor, rekindling her anger, which had evaporated when Mrs. Nelson entered. "I'm forming my own opinion, Aunt Flo."

"Hmph! One I obviously don't care for." She lifted her shoulder in a gesture of disapproval and turned to Elinor. "My dear, you don't have to listen to Lucas. He has a big bark, but he doesn't bite."

Elinor forced a polite smile even as she wanted to condemn the earl in front of the world. "We're discussing Christmas celebrations."

"Not one of Lucas's favorite subjects, if I recall. Somewhere along the way, he lost the Christmas spirit." She waved to Simon to join her. "Simon has asked me to invite you and the children for our festivities, and of course you can't say no." She glanced at Lucas. "I won't even bother to invite him."

"Mother, you're being excessively rude," Simon said. "Of course we'll invite Lucas. We also know he's going to decline because he has better things to do."

"Everyone is coming, close to fifty people—relations and good friends all, but I doubt we shall have room in my house for them." She glanced around the library as if deliberating.

"Mother, I know what you're thinking," Simon said in alarm. "'Twould be overwhelmingly cheeky to even suggest it."

"I was once Lady Florence Chandler, and I always will be, even if I married a Nelson."

As she continued, Simon closed his eyes and formed the next words silently as if he knew them by heart as she spoke. "This was once my home, and always will be." She looked from one to the other. "I wish to plan the largest gathering of the Christmas season, and I want it to happen here, where everyone in the family gathered once upon a time."

"I don't remember the event," Simon said.

"Well, you're just too young. It was before . . . before my brother turned cold and reclusive."

"When Edith died," Lucas said.

The words hung in the air like an accusation.

"Yes, dear nephew, when little Edith passed on. A most sad event, but it was wrong to grieve as long and hard as your parents did."

No one replied, and Elinor noticed the pain passing across the earl's face. He looked away, and she felt a wave of pity for him.

"Well?" Mrs. Nelson shouted. "What is it going to be Lucas, a new beginning? Or more of this dull life of yours?"

Lucas slapped a ledger on his desk closed and sighed. "You have taken me by surprise and can't expect me to respond without some thought."

"You might as well say no right now," Florence said. "If you are left to your own devices, you will turn down my request. All those gloomy thoughts will storm in and lay siege upon your mind."

"Be that as it may, this is now my house, and I shall do as I see fit."

Florence flung a glove at him. "Impossibly rude! I don't know what to do with you, Lucas. You're hopelessly stubborn, not to mention mutton-headed."

"It's not the first time I have been told," Lucas said, sounding exasperated.

"Then mayhap you can change people's opinion of you, Lucas."

Florence was nothing if not forceful and direct, Elinor thought.

"Annie shall go to your house for Christmas Day, Aunt Flo. I won't change my mind about celebrating a quiet holiday, no matter how much begging you do."

Florence's cheeks grew redder with real color, and she fought the condemning words that surely hovered on her lips.

"You are an old man before your time, Lucas. Why, I'm old enough to be your mother, but it's clear to see I'm younger at heart than you'll ever be if you continue in this vein."

"Botheration, Mother," Simon said in exasperation. "Do let him be. We've heard it all before." He went to a tray of bottles and poured himself a snifter of brandy. "Something to warm my insides. It's blistering cold outside."

"Obliged for your support, Coz," Lucas said drily. "I don't know why everyone has to concern themselves with me."

"Because we care, Lucas," Aunt Florence cried.

He looked somewhat ashamed at that.

Elinor was losing all patience with him.

Florence gripped Elinor's arm none too gently. "Let's go and see the children, my dear. I'm sure Alex has grown a few inches since I last saw him."

"In a few weeks? Hardly," Elinor replied, feeling confused. This whole Christmas business had made her upset. Why was the earl so stubborn and unreasonable?

"Lucas is the most obstinate and unyielding man I know. I don't understand why he still has to live in the past," Florence said as they walked upstairs. "He'll have to change, or life will turn against him."

Elinor thought about the ghosts and what they'd said to him. "It certainly will."

Florence took her hand and squeezed it. "We shall contrive somehow. We don't need Lucas's support. I just thought 'twould be a good idea to brighten up this dull place for the holidays."

"I agree with you completely."

The children greeted them with great ardor. Cook had given them gingerbread and warm milk, and the scents filled the bright room. A fire blazed merrily in the fireplace, and cheerful pictures that they'd painted adorned the walls.

Florence turned to Elinor. "I know, though, that you've brought light into this household, and for that, I'm grateful."

Eleven

Late that night, Elinor tossed and turned in her bed and finally got up to fetch some milk in the kitchen. She would heat it as warm milk was supposed to have sleep-inducing qualities. A slice of cake would not come amiss, either.

She pulled her robe around her and tied the sash. Carrying a lit candle in a brass candlestick, she stepped downstairs. The mansion lay in total silence, the cool air unmoving and close.

The quietude of the darkness almost frightened her in its intensity, but she suspected her overactive imagination magnified things. She also vividly remembered what the earl had told her about his encounter with the ghosts and wondered if she would be the next victim on their list.

Not that she had anything to scrutinize in her life—or did she? Sometimes one was blind to reality.

The hallway appeared to grow narrower as she neared the back regions of the house. She stepped downstairs and opened the kitchen door, and warmth and wonderful scents of food welcomed her.

Glancing around, she wondered if anyone else

had had the same idea as herself, but she saw no one. Everything was quiet, and the cat lay curled on a stool in front of the hearth. Cats always found the coziest spot in a house.

She went into the larder and found a pitcher of milk, from which she poured a hearty measure into a small pan. Placing it near the fire on a trivet, she knew it would heat up in no time.

She had spied a pie tin with a crisp linen napkin spread over it. When she looked under it, she found an apple pie sprinkled with sugar and cinnamon.

God bless Cook, she thought, and found the pie still felt slightly warm. The apple-and-spice aroma made her mouth water. Without any hesitation, she cut a wedge and poured some thick cream from a small pitcher over it.

Finding a fork, she sat down in Cook's wooden rocking chair in front of the hearth and adjusted a pillow behind her back. She raised her feet onto a stool by the fire, relishing the warmth that traveled up her legs immediately.

"This is so much better than tossing on my cold mattress," she told the cat, who only cocked one ear in response. It kept snoozing, whiskers twitching as if it also smelled the wonder of Cook's apple pie.

She finished the pie and poured the milk into a glass and sipped. It had reached perfect temperature and tasted almost as good as the pie.

Staring dreamily into the fire, she finished and leaned back. Perhaps she could snooze here for an hour. No one would be the wiser, and her feet would be toasty.

Before she knew it, her eyelids started drooping, and she wasn't sure if she was dreaming or awake. Everything became a pleasant blur. A light snore startled her for a moment until she realized it was her own.

The earl found her sleeping, her head tilted sideways, her mobcap on the floor, and her tresses flowing freely over her shoulders. He had never realized she had such rich wavy tresses of beautiful copper tones. They rivaled the gentle flames of the fire in color, and the light from the hearth blazed across her face, making her features magical.

He'd always thought she looked beautiful, but like this, her face young and unguarded, something in his heart was touched, and he struggled with these new emotions.

For nothing in the world did he want to be drawn in by another woman. Phoebe had been one mistake too many, and he would never open the door to that kind of pain again. Invariably love led to pain, didn't it?

He fought the sensation that fluttered in his heart and turned away abruptly. Deciding to retreat the way he'd come, he turned. The floorboards creaked under him, and the sound startled the sleeping beauty.

"My lord!" she cried breathlessly and clapped her hands to her mouth. She looked around as if to find her bearings and saw that her cap had fallen off. Blushing, she quickly wound her hair into a knot and stuffed it under the cap. There, the prim and proper Mrs. Browning was back.

"I didn't want to wake you, Elinor. You looked very peaceful in your sleep."

"I couldn't sleep, so I came down here for some warm milk."

"Always a good remedy—that is, if you don't like to drink brandy."

She shook her head. "No, I don't."

"You would have to drink a fair amount of it," he said. "And then you would be tipsy."

She smiled. "I'm silly enough as it is."

"I doubt that very much."

She stood. "I'll leave you alone. If you're hungry, I can highly recommend Cook's apple pie. 'Tis heavenly. Don't forget the cream."

"I'd rather you stayed," he said.

Surprise overtook her. "I was sure you'd be keen to avoid my company after today."

"It isn't anything I haven't heard already," he said. "Aunt Flo is very frank and she speaks *a lot*. Once she starts, it's difficult to stop the flow." He gave her a wry smile. "And she's always right, of course."

"Women usually are," she said, giving a smile in return. "Tell me, how come you're so much nicer at night?"

"The same reason you're much bolder at night."

"Bolder? Or just more courageous?"

"Bolder and softer. Less the schoolmistress."

"And what's a schoolmistress like?"

"Very proper, somewhat stiff, and used to marshalling people in a militant fashion, full of efficiency and information—which is freely given whether one asks for it or not."

"I see. You're very observant."

"Only when I want to be."

"Hmm. You find me interesting enough to warrant scrutiny?" Her heartbeat escalated alarmingly.

"Certainly." He walked to the larder and rummaged among the dishes. "I'm very hungry, as I missed dinner." He found bread and cold cuts, which he brought to the table.

Elinor fetched at plate and cutlery from the cupboard. Before long, he was taking big bites out of bread draped with slices of ham and mustard, and washing it all down with ale.

She thought he looked appealing with his hair tousled and beard stubble shading his face. Naturally, it was very improper to stand here in the middle of the night in her nightrail and stare at him.

Even if he wore a brocaded dressing gown that concealed most of him, she was well aware of the intimacy of the situation.

"You're staring at me," he said as he set down the ale.

"Your hair is standing straight up in the back of your head."

He immediately moved to smooth it down. "No, it isn't."

"I wished to see your reaction."

"That's wicked," he said and looked heavenward.

"Only paying you back for your observation about schoolmistresses." She clasped her hands primly in front of her.

"You always have to have the last word, don't you?"

"Schoolmistresses usually do," she replied.

"Yes, of course." He laughed.

"I'm delighted to see you in such good spirits, my lord. You must've looked deeply into the brandy bottle."

"You believe I can't be happy without it?"

"'Tis unlikely."

"For that sharp comment, I shall make you drink some with me. I'm sure Cook has some here for cooking. It probably won't be as good as what's served upstairs, but it'll do."

"Oh no, I don't drink brandy." She held up her hand as if it ward him off.

"You will tonight. I'm ordering you to."

"I only take orders about Annie's schooling—if that."

"We shall see." He went to the larder and came out shortly, holding a bottle triumphantly aloft.

"Are you sleepy, Elinor?"

She had to shake her head. His entrance earlier had made her wide awake.

"Nothing like brandy to bring on a restful night—or what's left of it."

"Then you should've been sleeping like a new-born baby."

"Ha! That's proof I didn't drink any brandy."

She didn't have a reply to that.

He poured a small glass for her and beckoned her toward the table. She wanted to refuse him, but somehow she couldn't. As if mesmerized, she went to him. His gaze followed her progress, his expression unreadable. He held out the glass to her, and she accepted it. He smiled and poured himself some.

"So that we can sleep," he said as if to remind her why they were drinking brandy in the wee hours of the night. He saluted her, and she sniffed the potent liquid.

"Drink it," he admonished and pushed her hand toward her lips.

She debated whether to argue, but found it easier just to comply. She was too tired to bandy words with him. She'd found him just as stubborn as herself, which wasn't exactly a compliment. The brandy burned all the way to her stomach.

She coughed, her eyes watering. He laughed, throwing his head back, and the surprise of seeing him like that stopped her coughing. "I . . . didn't . . . know it tasted so fiery," she gasped. She wiped her lips and swallowed hard to get the taste out of her mouth.

He downed his own glass, his eyes still dancing with mirth. To her chagrin, he didn't even make a face.

"Ahhh, splendid!" He proceeded to pour out some more, and offered her another measure, but she jerked away as if slapped.

"One is quite enough, Lucas." An unfamiliar warmth started spreading through her, and everything took on a golden shimmer. Everything and every thought seemed lighter, and she knew the brandy had affected her. She'd had the same feeling when she'd consumed too much wine with dinner, but nothing like this wave.

"I believe all the traces of the schoolmistress have disappeared." He tossed back another swallow, then set the bottle down.

"I truly cannot see where the schoolmistress leaves off and I begin. Other than a certain glow, I don't feel any different."

"But there's softness to your eyes that wasn't there before."

"Why do you care?" she asked. "You're a misogynist at heart."

"I miss the moments of pleasure which you can experience only with a woman. For instance, I would never care if Simon's eyes softened."

She laughed and sank down on a chair by the table. "I can see your point."

He continued to eat, never taking his gaze off her.

"You must miss your wife," she said, knowing she was treading dangerous water.

"I suppose it's time I tell you about Phoebe, since you're helping to raise her daughter."

"It may be helpful."

He leaned back in his chair, his hand lying motionless on the table. The mirth that had danced across his face faded, and she saw the specter of pain again lurking at the back of his eyes.

"Naturally, Phoebe was beautiful, the belle of the

Season," he began. "Everyone courted her and fawned over her. I was no different. I'd never been in love until I met Phoebe. Her face turned artists rapturous with praise. Her hair had the color of spun honey, and her shape was that of a delicate nymph. Her eyes—you should've seen her eyes—"

"Deep blue like Annie's, mayhap?" she inserted.

"No. Phoebe had sea green eyes, bottomless and, well, treacherous, like the currents that can drown you if swim too far out to sea."

Silence fell for a moment, and Elinor sensed the abyss into which they were about to descend.

"Due to my wealth and standing," he continued, "she treated me with special attention, and I knew I had won her hand when she agreed to allow me three dances at Almack's one night. By that she almost compromised herself, and I offered for her hand the very next morning. Her father, bless his soul, was more than happy to accept the generous offer. Phoebe would never lack for anything."

"Except maybe love," Elinor mused. "She never loved you back, did she?"

He shook his head. "I believed she did, and her reluctance to my touch I read as maidenly shyness, but the truth is she hated to have me near. Once we had consummated the marriage, she refused me completely, and it shook me to the very foundation of my being. I had thought I finally had a close companion, someone who would be my confidante and help me create a family, but she turned out to want only what my wealth could buy. I berated myself," he growled.

Elinor didn't respond. She longed to put her hand on his arm in consolation, but she didn't. He had to revisit that pain on his own, she reasoned. Surely he didn't expect her to console him.

"I considered myself a complete idiot for having been taken in by her beauty. I should've seen the lack of true depth. Phoebe was naught but a spoiled girl who never grew up."

"They say love is blind."

He didn't reply immediately, and she sensed his humiliation.

"Lucas, everyone makes mistakes."

"This was a blunder that created long-term ramifications."

"Did you reconcile yourself to the situation?"

"I spent many a night at my club, and I found myself beginning to loathe her. Then the whole world found out that she had a lover, Lord Swindon. The only reason she didn't marry him was because he always had pockets to let. She was in love with him the whole time."

"But Annie—"

"Swindon fathered Annie. I certainly know I didn't, and Annie has his coloring, the blond hair and blue eyes, the shape of his face and nose."

"That must've hurt," she said lamely.

"I wanted to kill him, and nearly did, but Phoebe swore she would kill *me* if I as much as touched a hair on his head. I'd never seen that ruthless side of her. I believe she would've killed me."

"And you let Swindon live."

"I couldn't bring more scandal to the family.

Everyone whispered about us, and I'm certain everybody knew about their duplicity before I did." He refilled his glass with brandy.

"I see now why you are alienated from Annie," she said simply.

He couldn't reply, but he nodded, his eyes haunted as he glanced at the leaping flames of the fire.

"Annie is innocent. She believes you're her father, and you are. She lives here, not at Lord Swindon's. He would no more acknowledge her than you do." Elinor took a deep breath. "She deserves better."

"I know that, but I can't deal with it."

"So as your heart is broken, you break her heart by ignoring her, again and again."

He wiped his hand across his face as if to remove some inner picture. "Every time I see her, I'm reminded of my anger. Every day I battle my desire to confront Swindon."

"Phoebe is no longer here, so there's in fact no rivalry. If I remember correctly, I heard he's about to marry a widow, someone rather older than he—"

"And who has very comfortable circumstances. He should be made to pay for the havoc he has wrought in people's lives, but instead, he's moving into a life of luxury."

"I can understand your resentment. However, Annie knows nothing about this, and she needs her father."

He pushed away from the table, his face twisted into a grimace of pain. "Don't repeat yourself, Elinor! Facing your accusing eyes every day since you moved here has been difficult enough. They have followed me in my dreams. I don't have to explain myself to you or restitute myself. All I'm doing is telling you about the past."

He paced the kitchen and pushed his hands through his hair. For a time she thought he would wipe everything from the table with an angry sweep of his arm, but he controlled himself.

"I'm grateful for the confidence," she said simply. "It means there's some kind of trust between us, and that's important to me."

He stopped before her. "Trust? I don't mean to trust another woman ever again, just as I don't plan ever to get leg-shackled again." He added with fierce intensity, "I'd rather go through the fires of hell than face another female in front of a clergyman."

Elinor laughed, then clapped her hand to her mouth.

He glowered at her.

"I'm sure Florence would've appreciated the drama of that statement."

"Aunt Flo? She's not part of this conversation."

"I'm sure she'd have plenty to say on the matter."

"She has said a great deal, much more than I ever care to listen to, and she's still harping on me every time I see her."

"She means well," Elinor said. "And you know that."

He nodded, but his impatience was easy to read. "She's the worst busybody."

"And lacks total deference to you."

He leaned his hands on the table and loomed over her. "She's completely disrespectful, and shows not one ounce of compassion."

"Woe is me." She burst out laughing again and realized the brandy had loosened her tongue. If she didn't take heed, she might say something she'd regret later.

"You can laugh all you want, but it only proves my point that females are flighty and untrustworthy. Not that I say you are with Annie or in your work—I have nothing to complain about—but you're as featherwitted as the rest of your sisters when it comes to more personal situations."

"I resent that immensely," she said, her ire kindled. "I went into my marriage with maturity and respect. I knew Matthew very well when we entered matrimony, and we got along. There was never a question in my mind about the suitability of our union."

"Steady as a rock, eh?"

"That he was, and so was our life together. If he hadn't met an untimely death, there's no doubt in my mind we would've been happy today."

He looked at her for a long time without saying anything.

"Furthermore, you're not the only one who has suffered. I grieved a great loss, and part of me died with Matthew, but I didn't turn bitter. I have confidence there's enough room in my heart for loving another husband, if that situation should ever be presented in my future."

"I don't doubt someone will find you very appealing." He sounded matter-of-fact and wore an expression that looked somewhat mutinous.

"Thank you," she said, inexplicably disappointed. Some of the pleasure had gone away with his statement, and she felt tired. "I believe the brandy has done its duty. My eyelids are finally drooping."

"Like lead, are they?" he said with an abrupt laugh.

She nodded. "Yours should be heavy as well."

"They are, but I'm unsettled inside."

"Any subject that stirs such violent emotions would keep you awake. Perhaps it would be easier to speak about it in broad daylight."

"'Tis never easy."

"And the night is softer and more forgiving, not as stark and revealing of the truth."

"One's own shortcomings don't seem too insurmountable in the dark."

"That may be true, but the demons of guilt and fear roam free at night, and are kept at bay by the comfortable and familiar daylight." She rose from the table. Startled, she watched as the door opened silently. For a moment she stared, and she gestured to the earl to look. Perhaps the ghosts were afoot.

She saw nothing but darkness at first. Then something moved and came closer. Her heartbeat raced. She almost expected to see a specter standing beyond.

Twelve

Two small figures emerged from the black hallway, and Elinor gasped. "Annie! Alex! What in the world? Where's Nanny?"

"Asleep," Annie replied as she stepped inside hesitantly. Her white nightgown dragged along the floor, and the nightcap tied under her chin with ribbons sat askew on her blond curls. Alex looked wide awake as he ran past her and threw himself into Elinor's arms.

"Mama, I didn't know where you were."

She hugged him. "Why are you two up in the middle of the night?"

"I couldn't sleep, and then I waked Annie to play. She said she was cold."

Annie ran forward and hugged Elinor's waist. She peered uncertainly at the earl, who still stood by the table. Elinor exchanged a glance with him that begged him to greet the children.

"We're hungry, Mama," Alex said when he discovered the leftover bread and meat on the table.

"You can have some milk and pie," she replied and released their arms from her body. "Go sit down."

The earl pulled out chairs and the children sat down. Annie looked up at him with questions in her eyes, but he didn't say anything.

"Papa, can't you sleep?"

The earl's gaze darted from the child to Elinor and back. "No . . . I couldn't sleep tonight."

"I dreamed I was building a snowman, Mama." Alex took a bite out of the earl's leftover bread.

"Put that down, Alex." Elinor placed a pan of milk near the fire. "You'll have some warm milk shortly."

"I don't like milk," he replied peevishly.

Elinor tied napkins around their necks and pushed the chairs snug against the table. She fetched two small slices of pie and put them before the children. "I doubt you'll complain about Cook's apple pie."

They ate without objection.

She watched them and shook her head in exasperation. "I doubt I'll find peace any time soon tonight," she said to the earl with a laugh.

"It looks futile," he said.

They watched the children eat, and Elinor sensed the earl's frustration.

"Mrs. Browning, I want an apple," Annie said.

With a sigh, she went in search of an apple and found one in a basket in the larder. The fresh smell of fruit's red skin enticed her. She split it and gave each child one half.

The earl stood irresolutely in the middle of the room. "I suppose it's time to go upstairs," he said.

"Please stay," she said, hoping he would spend

some time talking to the children. "The gathering is growing by the hour. Before long the whole household might join us here."

"Heaven forfend!" the earl said and downed some more brandy. He pondered, staring at the children, then noticed the milk had started to rise in the pan. As Elinor put down the pie on the table, he hurried forward to rescue the milk from boiling over. Gripping the handle with an apron, he carried it away from the fire.

Elinor found two mugs and poured the milk, which she set on the table. "Perhaps you can tell them a story. That'll make them sleepy."

"Yes, Papa, tell us a story. Please." Annie gave the earl a beseeching glance.

"I . . . don't know," the earl said.

"Yes," Elinor said, "tell us a tale."

He gave her a look that said "traitor," and she shrugged her shoulders.

"I have forgotten all tales."

"You can always invent one," she insisted.

The earl looked trapped, but he finally sat down at the table. Toying with his brandy glass, he spun a tale of pirates on the seven seas.

Elinor listened to his halting story, and the children paid attention rapturously, especially Annie. Elinor prayed he would pay some attention to the girl. Perhaps tonight would be the night when their relationship would change to something more.

She glanced at the clock on the mantelpiece. Three o'clock. This was highly irregular, and if the servants got wind of this night's adventure, gossip would fly from door to door.

Yawning, she thought with yearning for her bed, but it seemed distant at this point. Unless the children fell asleep right away, she would have no rest. And now their eyes sparkled as they listened to the story. Sleep seemed far away.

The earl had forgotten his discomfort as he traveled through the lurid tale with the children, and Elinor concentrated on cleaning off the crumbs spilled on the table.

Just as the earl was about to finish, she heard a knock on the back door that faced the mews. Who in the world would be knocking on the door here in the dead of night? She debated what to do as the earl got up.

"I'd better see what is going on," he said, and opened the door just as another knock sounded.

Outside stood a ragged lot of beggars. An old man who could barely walk led the group of four, two women and two men, all rather long in the tooth. "'Ave mercy, yer 'ighness," he wheezed. "We're starvin', and we 'ave nuffin' to eat."

Elinor saw the bundles of rags that constituted their clothes and she wanted to give them some of hers. It always hurt to see the abject poverty in the city. What surprised her was that they had dared to approach a mansion in Grosvenor Square.

"Do you know someone here?"

They looked guilty. "Me cousin said she would put somethin' aside tonight. Didn't 'xpect strangers," the old man said, shuffling his feet.

"Who's your cousin?" the earl asked, his expression severe.

Elinor hoped he wouldn't deny them.

"Elsie Miller, the cook. Me mother's sister's youngest. Went far in life, Elsie did." The old man gave them a toothless grin. He put his grimy cap back onto his head. "Sorry to 'ave bothered you. We'll be on our way."

Elinor held her breath.

The earl opened the door wider. "On a perishing night like this, I can't deny you something warm. Come in."

"Are ye the butler then, yer 'ighness?" the old man said, making his slow way into the kitchen.

Your highness? the earl mouthed to Elinor. She wanted to laugh, but kept her mirth to herself.

"No, I'm one of the footmen," the earl lied.

The ragged group looked around them in awe. The women, whose noses were red with cold, moved to the fire, where they held out their hands.

To her surprise, the earl offered the old men some brandy. The children looked wide-eyed at the newcomers, and Elinor knew they were burning with questions. Alex began to open his mouth, but she quieted him with an admonition.

She urged the dirty and foul-smelling lot to sit down, then went to find some bowls. In a pot waited some leftover meat-and-vegetable soup, and Elinor suspected this was what Cook had saved for her poor relation and his friends.

She wondered what the earl would have to say to Cook in the morning. This could be an issue that would terminate her employment, but Elinor would have to put in a word in her favor. Why should anyone be punished for helping starving people?

She spooned soup into the bowls and cut up wedges of bread and cheese, then put the food before the people. The earl had, to her relief, poured ale in tankards for them. He couldn't be that set against helping if he served these poor souls.

"'Tis mighty gen'rous of you," one of the women said. "The owner of this pile 'as a terrible reputation."

The earl's eyebrows rose and he glanced at Elinor. For a moment a shadow moved across his face. "Why?" he asked.

"'E's a cold one, they say. Niver a smile, niver a kind word to an'one."

"Humbug," the earl replied.

"Perhaps he has a reason for it," Elinor said in defense of Lucas.

"Be that as it may," the woman said as she spooned the soup into her toothless mouth, "'tis said 'e's dimwitted and locked in the attic."

"Who has spread such rumors?" Elinor demanded.

"Oh, 'tis well known. 'Is 'ighness is a looby, an' no mistake about it."

"But you're willing to take his food?" the earl asked, crossing his arms across his chest.

"Cook pays for it from 'er wages," said the old man, who claimed to be her cousin.

"Hmm, she does?" the earl repeated.

Elinor found a basket behind the door filled with bread, wheels of cheese, a leg of mutton, and small meat pies. This must've been what she'd planned to give them to take home. "When did she expect you to appear to claim your basket?" she asked.

"Around nine, but we couldn't get 'ere on time," the old man said. "Got slowed by the weather. 'Tis snowin' 'ard outside."

"So I noticed," the earl said. "What else are people saying about Lord Lyons?"

"Bumped orf 'is wife, din't 'e?" the other woman said.

"What!" the earl yelled, and everyone jumped.

Elinor put her hands over Annie's ears so that the girl couldn't hear the rest. The child squirmed to get free, but Elinor admonished her to sit still.

"That young wife died tragically," the Cook's cousin said. "Of a broken 'eart."

"'E must've been a right ogre to 'er," the woman sitting next to him said.

"There are always two sides to a story," Elinor inserted.

They stared at her between bites of bread. "Aye, she wus the belle of London, wusn't she? She could've 'ad an'one she liked."

"She chose to marry into wealth," the earl growled.

"Me, I don't blame 'er," the other woman said, her bony chin bobbing.

Elinor could see her point, but she wondered who'd spread the information about Phoebe's broken heart. The servants chatted constantly.

"Poor thing," the old man muttered as he spooned the rest of the soup into his mouth.

"Before you start crying over her, let me inform you she was the most vain and selfish creature alive," the earl said.

Silence hung for a while as everyone digested that piece of information. The old men murmured something to each other.

"Ye must be a friend o' 'is lordship," Cook's cousin said. "I daresay 'e needs a friend, seein' as 'e 'as nobody."

The earl looked startled by the comment, and Elinor thought he might get angry, but he only retreated into himself. The statement was almost true. The earl had his family, but she hadn't seen many friends around.

"They call 'im the curmudgeon of Grosvenor Square," one of the women supplied.

Elinor glanced at Lucas. He didn't appear pleased, which was understandable.

The old people finished their meal and thanked Elinor profusely. She showed them the basket and gave them some shiny apples to add to their meal. Then she asked them to wait while she fetched two of her old shawls and gave them to the women.

"Yer ever so kind, missus," they said and shuffled to the door as they admired their new clothing with pleasure. Wrapping themselves up, they went into the snowy night.

Lucas closed the door behind them. "A very illuminating experience," he said.

"What's a cur-mugg-in?" Annie asked, all eyes.

"Someone who is cross all the time, and mostly alone because he doesn't have many friends."

"Are you that, Papa?" she asked, her little face worried.

The earl's shoulders slumped. Elinor held her breath, wondering if he would deny it—lying to himself.

"I suppose I am, Annie," he said.

It was the first time Elinor had heard him use Annie's name, and it pleased her more than she could describe. This night had been a great blessing, including the revelations the poor people had brought. To become a more open and forgiving man, it might be good that he heard what people had to say about him.

He raked his hands through his hair until he looked wild. His face was set, and Elinor couldn't read his thoughts.

"Finish your milk, children. Then it's back to bed." She cleared off the table, making sure all bowls and dishes were stacked in the scullery and all spills and crumbs wiped off. Cook would wonder who had marauded the larder, but she would also notice the basket was gone. Tomorrow would be a day for explanations, she thought.

The earl wished them all good night. "I shall talk to you tomorrow," he said to Elinor.

She nodded and watched as Annie waved at her father. Elinor hoped he would respond, but he didn't.

Thirteen

The days moved closer to Christmas.

You can really feel the excitement in the air, Elinor thought as she looked out the window one morning. Big fluffy white swags of snow lined every windowsill, and the mounds along the street still had that clean white-blue look after the recent snowfall. It promised to be a long and cold winter.

She hadn't seen the earl since their midnight foray into the kitchen, and the children hadn't mentioned the event. They had promptly fallen asleep and anything that had happened that night must've appeared as a dream to them.

Cook confessed to feeding her cousin on occasion, and it was true she paid for it out of her own pocket. One bright progress came out of that as the earl—Elinor had heard—had given his consent to foot the bill for any food she might be donating to the needy. He had even suggested that the poor elderly cousin collect a feast for Christmas, and lots of baskets were being packed in the kitchen. The spirit of giving had infected everyone.

Elinor conferred with Mrs. Braithewaite, who ordered baskets of holly and mistletoe to adorn the many mantelpieces and lintels of the house. The greenery brought the freshness of the outdoors inside, and as the footmen opened the big front doors to sweep the snow off the steps, a gust of wind flew inside to stir the still and gloomy air.

"That's what it needs," Elinor said to the butler as he walked by in the hallway.

"Beg your pardon?"

"The house needs to be aired out."

The butler looked unsure. "Madam, the temperatures—"

"Yes, I know it's cold, Winslow, but even just for a few moments." She followed the butler to the kitchen, where a basket of fresh oranges awaited her attention. The children were already there, stuffing their mouths with warm gingerbread and looking very happy.

"You know what to do, children. Push the cloves into the oranges." She pushed the bowl of cloves toward them.

"I shall make an extra nice one for Papa," Annie said. "For his desk."

Elinor's heart pinched at the words. No progress with the earl had come out of the night he'd spent with the little ones. Annie was trying desperately to please him, and Elinor wanted to shake him to make him face the truth, but he'd been unreachable since that night. She had waited the entire following day to be summoned to his library, but nothing had happened. Either he'd forgotten, or he was avoiding her.

She sighed, feeling disappointed. Her hopes had been dashed.

The children worked diligently, the kitchen filling up with the cheerful and reviving scent of orange. They ate part of their project, and Elinor shared in the bounty. Fresh oranges soothed one's soul, she thought as she savored a juicy section.

The milk wagon delivered milk, the butcher packets of meat, and the Cook bent over a box of sugartops and spices that had been some of the things to arrive, all for making special dishes for Christmas. More exotic fruits arrived in crocks. Elinor watched dried figs and plums appear, and even dried berries found their way to Cook's larder.

"Nothing but the best," Cook said. "We're not going to 'ave a sad Christmas like last year. 'Is lordship didn't touch a thing I made. 'E slept most of the day away, and we ended up eating sweetmeats in the servants' 'all until we suffered from a severe belly ache." She placed her fat hands on her hips. "'Tis not goin' to 'appen agin this year."

"I believe the earl is in a better frame of mind this Christmas," Elinor said.

"I know if I arsk 'im agin what 'e would like on 'is table for Christmas, 'e won't 'ave any suggestions."

"Be that as it may, I won't allow it. For the children's sake, we're going to have a lovely Christmas, and if Mrs. Nelson has her way, most of the family will celebrate here."

"That'll be the day! 'Is lordship will dig 'is 'eels in, you mark me words."

"Elsie, he may be outnumbered this year. There's

power in numbers. Simon will be on my side, and he doesn't give up easily."

"Mr. Nelson is as nice as a man can be," the cook said, her gaze calculating. "If ye play yer cards right, Mrs. Browning, ye might be able to nab 'im for a 'usband."

Elinor blushed at such forthright speech. She knew Cook had a point. *The sad part is I don't have any interest in Simon, other than as a friend,* she thought. "He's a good man, but not for me."

"Ye can't remain on the shelf, Mrs. Browning." The cook hefted a great urn and put it on the table.

"I'm not concerned about that," Elinor said, wishing to change the subject.

"Mama shall marry a man with many horses," Alex said.

Elinor laughed. "I know you're interested in horses, Alex, but I see no reason why you should need more than one."

"First I have to learn how to ride."

Elinor felt a pang of guilt that Alex didn't have a pony. She had learned how to ride on a docile pony at Alex's age. "Mayhap Mr. Nelson will teach you how to ride when the weather improves. He has a great many horses, I believe."

"Then you should marry him, Mama."

"I wish life were that simple," Elinor said, still laughing. Out of the mouths of babes . . .

"The master could use a wife," the cook continued as she scooped butter into small balls and put them on gilt-edged dishes.

"No one wants to marry Papa," Annie piped up.

She kept her concentration on the orange in her hand, but her little face looked sad.

"Why?" Alex demanded. "He has a big house and horses."

"Papa is angry all the time. His wife wouldn't be happy."

Elinor thought it shrewd of the girl to discern such facts, but then she had firsthand knowledge of the emotion. For her young age, she'd suffered a lot of rejection.

"We could tell him a story and cheer him up," Alex suggested and licked orange juice off his fingers. "Just like he did for us."

"'Twould have to be a happy story, then," Annie said.

"'E told you a story?" Cook asked, her eyes round with surprise.

Elinor prayed they wouldn't mention they had all been in the kitchen wearing nothing but their nightrails.

"We couldn't sleep and he told us a tale about evil pirates," Alex said. "I want to be a pirate when I grow up."

"No, you don't," Cook said with a huff. She buttered pieces of muffin and placed them in front of each child. "Pirates steal, drink cheap gin, and are a foul-mouthed lot. Nothing ye want to be, Master Alex."

"I could travel on a big ship all over the world," Alex continued, his face alight with imagination.

"Some other pirate is liable to cut yer 'ead orf," Cook said without preamble.

"I shall carry a big sword and cut his off first."

"Ha! Ye're a bloodthirsty one, aren't ye?"

"Blood makes my stomach funny," Alex said at last.

"There ye go then! Yer not fit for piracy, and a blessing it is."

Elinor shook her head in wonder. The children got along so well with the rest of the servants, and she did as well. These people had easily become her new family.

"I'm goin' to make marzipan animals for you. You can have a whole stable of them."

"I want horses only," Alex cried.

Cook rolled her eyes heavenward, and Elinor laughed.

"Stallions, mares, geldings, foals, and ponies," Alex continued.

"Now, 'ow do I tell 'em apart?" Cook asked shrewdly. She waited for his reply, and Elinor realized she'd never taught Alex the difference.

"Stallions are big, and mares are smaller." He screwed up his face as if concentrating hard. "Geldings are stallions that don't have . . . that can't . . . that have missing parts," he explained.

"Who told you that?" Elinor asked.

"His lordship. He has a great big gelding, a chestnut with a white blaze and a black mane. I wanted to ride it, and he said he might let me some day."

"You're not supposed to be in Lord Lyons's way. How many times have I told you, Alex?"

"He didn't mind. I was outside making snowballs with Nanny when he rode up. He let me sit in the saddle for a while. The horse went funny and wanted to run away, but the earl controlled him."

"Much too spirited by the sound of it," Elinor said. "You need a gentle horse to learn on."

"I want to learn riding, too," Annie said and braced her elbows on the table. "My mother knew how to ride."

"Do you remember her well?"

Annie shook her head. "No."

The door opened and Winslow entered, carrying an empty silver tray. "His lordship wishes a cup of coffee. Is there any left?"

Cook went to look in the pot. "'E'll have to make do with what's left. I'm not about to start something fresh at this time of morning."

"How irreverent of you, Elsie," the butler said. "I'll make some for him."

"Always on 'is side, aren't ye, Winslow?" Cook muttered. "What is 'e doing anyway?"

"Correspondence."

"Must be writing Christmas letters to the friends 'e doesn't 'ave," Cook said with more irreverence. "That is if 'e's not too stingy to frank the envelopes."

"Elsie!" the butler admonished.

"He's not a skinflint," Elinor interjected.

Later in the day Alex got up from the school table and went to climb up a chair to look out the window. "Mama, the sun is shining. Can we go outside?"

Elinor thought it might be a good idea to get

some fresh air and exercise. "Very well, let's go find your cloaks. 'Tis cold outside."

The children ran through the house shouting at each other, and Elinor admonished them, but they didn't heed her. She helped them lace up their thick boots and don coats and cloaks, mittens and scarves. She tied a red bonnet over Annie's blond curls and tossed Alex a knit cap. Then she made herself ready. The outing excited her. They had been inside far too long waiting for the snow to stop falling.

The winter sun looked pale and weak, but it reflected off the snow, creating a fairy landscape of white and diamonds. Snow draped the black branches like soft rabbit fur, and made every bush into round mounds, hiding thorns and sharp twigs with brittle down.

"Mama, I can hit that tree from here," Alex cried, aiming a snowball at a nearby trunk. He let it fly, and did indeed hit his target with a *plop*.

"Well done, Alex," she called out.

Annie tried, but her aim was not as accurate, which annoyed her. She always tried to emulate Alex, and her frustration was great when she fell short.

Elinor saw the earl's coach coming from the mews and halting in front of the house. He must be going somewhere, she thought. Alex ran to speak to the groom holding the horses, and eagerly stroked the soft muzzles.

The square looked rather empty. The gentry had departed London for their country estates weeks ago, but there had been no mention of the earl vacating his London home. She suspected he didn't want to rattle around his great estate in Kent without anyone to talk to but the servants all winter.

The huge front doors opened, and the earl stepped out dressed in a coat, beaver hat, and gloves. Due to the heavy snow, he wore topboots rather than his polished Hessians. He looked elegant and impressive and so remote—quite a different character than the man she'd spoken with in the kitchen.

"Papa," Annie yelled, but she didn't run forward. She clung to Elinor's cloak and looked at him from the distance.

Elinor gripped her hand and squeezed it. "Your father might be in a hurry, Annie. We can't take up his time." She prayed the earl would acknowledge the children. He'd stopped as he heard Annie. *Oh, please God, if You're at all merciful, make him say something.*

Fourteen

"Annie," he said, his face stiff and void of emotion, but Elinor sensed that he struggled inside. "Hello."

"My lord," cried Alex. "Can I ride one of your horses soon?"

He turned his attention on the boy. "That's always a possibility—if you can let go of your mother's apron strings." He took off his hat to greet Elinor. "Mrs. Browning. I'm glad to see you in such fine fettle—wholly rested, I hope, after your recent bout of insomnia."

"Yes, thank you," she said, her voice breathless. Why did his presence always make her heart race?

"Alex is going to become a pirate, Papa," Annie said from the folds of Elinor's cloak.

"You need to grow big and strong first, Alex," the earl said. "To do that, you need to eat lots of Cook's pies and sweetmeats."

Alex whooped and danced around, and Elinor smiled. "You've made him very happy." She hoped he would say something equally kind to Annie, but he ignored her.

"I decided to deliver some papers to my solicitor's office. If you care to, we can stop at Burlington Arcade and see what the shops have to offer," he said.

"The children would like that," she said.

"You wouldn't?" he asked.

She blushed, wondering if he understood how her heart made somersaults in his presence. "I would."

"I haven't met a female who doesn't like to shop," he said with a laugh.

They piled into the coach, and the earl spread rugs over their legs to keep the chill out. The children looked out the window and commented on ice-skaters on a tiny pond and ducks sitting in the snow as if watching the activity.

"Where will they swim?" Annie wondered.

"They can fly to the river," Elinor explained.

The earl smiled, but he avoided looking at Annie.

"Cook says we're going to have lots of food for Christmas," Alex explained to the earl.

"Ducks?"

The children stared at him wide-eyed, and when they noticed that he was smiling, they giggled.

The sun was moving below the rooftops, sending an orange glow over everything. Elinor thought the earl looked very handsome with that unworldly light across his face. She realized she'd missed him since their encounter in the kitchen.

Had he missed her? *Hardly,* she thought. *Why would he?* He had confided in her in a weak moment, but she had been there when he needed someone. It could have been anyone. Cook or one of the upstairs maids . . . no, of course not, she admonished herself. He wouldn't divulge his secrets to the servants. Then again, she was a servant now. She had to remember that.

She floundered in a moment of confusion.

"You're unusually quiet," he said to her, and scrutinized her face. "Which surprises me. As long as I've known you, you've had plenty to say."

"Sometimes all of us fall into pensive moods," she replied evasively. She glanced out the window to avoid his penetrating look, but she felt it on her for the longest time. Part of her knew she couldn't hide from him.

"Some more than others. That mood can take over if we aren't careful," he said.

She nodded.

"I noticed all the holly and mistletoe all over the house," he said. "As far as I know, I never asked for any of that."

"Everyone knows that, but we took it upon ourselves to make your home a bit livelier. If you don't like it, you'll have to order us to take it down, but I'm certain you won't."

She gave him a hard stare, and this time he looked away.

"No, but I'm surprised at the servants' gall. There must be an instigator among you."

"What's an insti-ga-tor?" Annie asked.

"Someone who starts mischief or someone who convinces others to do things even if they don't want to," Elinor explained. "Sometimes that can be good, but more often than not, it's bad."

"We have a bad insti-ga-tor at home?" she asked.

The earl chuckled and Elinor laughed. "No, not at all. There are only good people at home, people who want to make others happy at Christmas," she said.

"Yes!" Annie cried. "I want to be happy, and I want you to be happy," she added, and slid her hand shyly into Elinor's.

Elinor squeezed it gently, and the earl watched the exchange, no doubt feeling uncomfortable. Elinor knew Annie longed to slide her hand into his, but it would be a long time before she dared. Only when she knew he wouldn't reject her would she do it.

"Mrs. Braithewaite is making a doll for me. She has a beautiful evening gown of pink silk," Annie said to her father. "Her hair is red, just like Mrs. Browning's."

"Real hair?" Elinor asked. "Is that why some of mine is missing at the back?"

Annie giggled. "No! Mrs. Braithewaite is using silk thread. It's ever so shiny."

"Just like yours, then. Yours is as shiny as the moon," Elinor said kindly.

Annie laughed with delight.

"And Mrs. Browning's is like polished copper," the earl said, a strange note in his voice.

"Thank you," she whispered, light-headed for a moment. He had actually paid her a compliment.

"I had a cat once named Copper," Alex said, then returned to his vigil by the window.

Darkness was falling rapidly at this time of year. It was no later than four o'clock, and already the lamps were being lit outside the houses. The streets were still filled with wagons, and people carrying trays and baskets. The vendors were going home to find solace before fires.

"And Mrs. Browning's eyes are blue like the sea," the earl added, "sometimes a stormy gray, sometimes green, sometimes glinting and smiling as when the sun plays over the water."

Elinor could not believe her ears.

"When she's angry, they are almost black," he continued.

"I never knew," she replied.

Annie looked doubtful. "Her eyes are blue, Papa."

"But not as blue as yours, Annie," she said. "You have the most heavenly blue eyes."

Annie's face shone with pleasure as they passed a light that sent a beacon into the carriage. "Do you think so, Papa?"

Before he could reply, Alex made a noise, evidently having had enough poetry to last him for a long time.

"Do you have something to say, Alex?" Elinor asked, her voice stern to hide her inner confusion.

"No, Mama. You're being silly."

"Nonsense. We're playing with words."

"And feelings," the earl said sotto voce.

"I don't understand completely," she replied,

and she didn't. Why had he suddenly chosen to give her compliments?

"Don't all of us sometimes get caught up in flights of fancy?" he said, and she sensed he wanted to say more but couldn't before the children.

"Yes, I suppose." She heaved a deep sigh and squared her shoulders to get back her sense of reality. "'Tis good you're going out with us, my lord, and I'm grateful for your company."

"We'll be silly this evening," he suggested.

"You must have found a particularly good label of brandy this afternoon," she said to confuse the young ears directed toward them with interest.

"It was an old one, mellow and quite smoky. I enjoyed a small measure, but not to the point where I lost myself."

"I see." She didn't know what more to say. The man reminded her of an eel, something she couldn't quite get a grip on. "So you don't mind the mistletoe," she continued.

"I shall take full advantage of it at the earliest opportunity," he replied, again startling her when she thought the compliments were over. She trod on dangerous ground here.

"Mama, we're stopping," Alex cried with enthusiasm. All he wanted was to spend time with the horses. He turned to the earl. "May I talk to the grooms while you're—"

"Yes, you may," the earl interrupted.

He had barely uttered the words before Alex had jumped down and rushed to see about the horses. The earl shook his head in wonder. He took an en-

velope from the seat and stepped out of the carriage. "I'll only be a moment."

They waited and Elinor could hear Alex chatting
animatedly. Annie touched her hand again. "Mrs.
Browning, you're the bestest gov-er-ness," she said,
stumbling over the last word. "I wish you were my
mama."

Elinor closed her eyes for a moment, feeling the
tears burning behind her eyelids. "Oh, Annie,
you're so sweet."

"I don't remember my mama, but I miss her."

Elinor patted Annie's cheek. "I'm sure you do. I
miss mine too."

"She's with the angels, too?"

Elinor nodded. "Yes."

"Mayhap they are together. Do you think they
are?"

"All I know is that they must be angels, but I have
no clue whether they are together or not."

"Do you think all the angels know each other?"

"They probably do, Annie—if not by name, by
feeling."

She thought about that for a moment, and Elinor wished it were true. She hoped Phoebe had
found peace.

They sat in silence for some time. Alex was chattering outside incessantly. After a few minutes, the
earl returned. As he entered the coach, the tension
returned, and Elinor took a deep breath to steady
herself.

Alex was full of news about the horses, as if something momentous had changed since they started

out. "They were groomed this morning and had their hooves polished," he said excitedly. "And they were fed oats."

"With the weather so severe, they grow fat and lazy in the stables," the earl commented.

"They don't look fat, my lord, and their hooves are dirty again from the mud."

The earl laughed. "You're right, of course."

They arrived shortly at the Burlington Arcade, where the shops were lit up with oil lamps and candles. This was not a fashionable hour for shopping, but Elinor had come to understand that the earl rarely followed convention about protocol.

"How about visiting that shop?" the earl suggested, pointing at a window filled with gewgaws and toys.

The children were delighted and wanted to rush in immediately, but Elinor kept a firm hand on theirs. The little shop was pure enchantment, with brightly painted wooden toys and dolls that wore dresses embroidered with silver and gold. The children wanted everything they saw and kept exclaiming in wonder.

"This could become tiresome," the earl murmured. "Let's find a less tempting emporium."

The shopkeeper, a short older man, bowed gratefully as the earl asked him to wrap up a small wooden soldier for Alex and a carved cat with a pink bow for Annie. The children thanked Lucas rapturously for the gifts.

Annie held on to her package and wouldn't let go. Elinor knew it was the first gift the earl had ever given her. He was changing, and the realization filled her with new hope. Mayhap Annie would have a father after all.

"I need maps for the schoolroom," Elinor said. "The book shop might have some."

"Geography always made me dream of exotic lands," he said.

"Where it never snows," she supplied.

"And elephants walk on the streets."

Alex was all ears. "Elephants?"

They went into a discussion about the massive animals, and Elinor enjoyed listening. Alex needed a father, too, that much was clear, and she needed a partner. She couldn't harbor those thoughts, not now. Not when she felt her heart pounding because of Lucas's proximity. It just wouldn't do to have any kind of feelings or hopes about him. Besides, he had many emotional problems.

Oh, what to do? she thought, frustrated. Perhaps she should accept Simon's courtship. It was clear she hadn't many opportunities anymore to meet someone else. But she didn't have romantic feelings for Simon. She glanced at the earl and knew in her heart she had feelings for him, and the knowledge frightened her no end.

Despite his romantic, poetic words to her, she sincerely doubted he *could* love her. Beside the bitterness in his heart, there was precious little room for romance.

Fifteen

The earl must've been in an extravagant mood, because he bought twists of mints and paper cones of sweets for the children. She noticed he didn't buy anything for her, except for the maps at the booksellers. It wasn't as if she expected anything, not really, but part of her wanted some small token. Then again, she could not see herself buying something for him.

Her reverie shattered as she heard male voices greeting the earl. She glanced at the trio of gentlemen dressed in drab coats and beaver hats. Elegance stood written in every detail of their appearance, from their flawless neckcloths to their polished boots.

She recognized Lord Swindon and the other two, portly middle-aged men she'd seen at functions, but she didn't know them personally. She stiffened as she noticed the contempt on Lord Swindon's handsome face. His eyes were hard and somewhat bloodshot, from what she could see.

"The recluse of Grosvenor Square," he drawled. "I never dreamed I'd see you in the Burlington Arcade."

"Not exactly one of your regular haunts either, Swindon. Low gaming hells are more your style."

Tension hung thick, and Elinor worried they would come to blows. The children came running after staring at a monkey on the shoulder of a man playing a hurdy-gurdy. She gripped their hands and quieted them with a sharp, "Hush!"

Swindon stared as if mesmerized at Annie. Elinor knew he hadn't seen the child for a long time, if ever. Annie moved closer to Elinor's side, hiding in the fold of her cloak.

"I see you're in the middle of a family outing," he said, his voice cold. "That explains the shopping. Not that I've ever known you to be extravagant, Lyons. Rather the opposite."

"Not that it's any of your business, Swindon," the earl said, his voice as icy.

Swindon's gaze roamed from Annie to Elinor and back. "The girl looks just like me," he said.

Elinor gasped and pressed Annie closer. She prayed the child hadn't understood the meaning of his comment. The earl stiffened beside her, a coiled spring ready to lash out. She touched his arm. "Let's just move on, my lord."

"And who is this, calling you 'my lord?'"

"No one you'll ever know," the earl growled.

"Whoever she is, she's beautiful. If you don't want to introduce us, I'll find someone who does. You know I can be very determined."

"All for the wrong reasons. You bring nothing but misery into people's lives."

"That's a very subjective view, Lyons. I know any number of people who will vouch for me."

"Then those people don't have very good judgment."

"Here now!" one of Swindon's companions said. "I will not accept such insults upon my character."

"Nor will I," said the other man pompously.

"There's no reason to get into an argument," Elinor said, trying to soothe the rough waters.

"There's all the reason," the earl said. "I can't speak for other people, but I know what you did to me and mine—"

"No one was forced into anything," Swindon said, looking down his nose, even if the earl stood several inches taller. "I can't be blamed for actions others choose."

Elinor sensed the earl's anger boiling to the surface. He would explode any minute, and Elinor didn't want the children to witness the wrath. Alex was all ears as it was, and Annie was still hiding.

"Gentlemen—" she started.

Swindon slid his eyes toward her, the calculation in his expression evident.

"She *is* beautiful, this mystery woman of yours, and if she's available and willing—"

The earl slapped him across the face. "She's not available, you cur," he said between clenched teeth. "You'll pay for your insolence to her."

Swindon's companions drew in audible breaths. "You just challenged him, Lyons."

"I guess I did," the earl said in a low, angry voice.

"Name your seconds. We shall meet at your earliest convenience."

Elinor couldn't believe her eyes. Why had this had to happen this afternoon? They had been having such a wonderful time, and the children had been enjoying themselves as they hadn't done in days, even weeks.

"Gentlemen," she admonished, her voice the most schoolmistressish she could make it, "'tis Christmas in a few days. 'Tis a celebration of peace. You can't mean to—"

"Stay out of this, Elinor," the earl snapped, turning his ire on her.

"Oooh, she has a name," Swindon drawled. "Elinor. What a lovely name."

The earl looked as if he could tear Swindon in half with his bare hands. Elinor couldn't stand the tension. She started to move away, pulling the children with her. Without looking to see if the earl would follow, she went into a shop that sold coffees and teas. Big barrels sent out an enticing aroma, and Elinor spied some chocolate bonbons under a domed glass lid. She pointed them out to the children, who immediately wanted some. Pulling out her purse, she made a purchase just as the earl entered. She still sensed his anger, but at least the men hadn't come to blows in the street.

"Was that necessary?" she whispered to Lucas as the shop owner engaged Annie and Alex in conversation. She felt completely unsettled and angry.

"Of course it was," he said. "The man insulted you."

"This has nothing to do with me," she hissed. "'Tis all about the past."

"He even had the gall to place his beady eyes on Annie."

"As if you cared," she shot back.

That silenced him, and his mouth pinched into a thin line. He looked unnaturally pale, and his eyes were so stormy she thought he would scream at her or shake her, but he didn't move.

"I wish I did," he said finally. "You don't know what it's like to live in an ice fortress."

"One you built yourself," she said, wishing she could shake some sense into him.

"Be that as it may, I didn't know better."

"And you do now?"

"I'm beginning to, thanks to you and the ghosts."

"It took something from the other world to move you as well as to make you think. I find that disturbing."

"Again, I didn't know better, but I'm beginning to understand, and I'm sorry for all time that I've lost—"

"Wallowing in self-pity."

"That says a lot about my enormous pride," he said with a sigh. He looked very tired all of a sudden. "'Tis not pleasant for me to see myself."

"Confrontation never is, but I don't see a need for revenge. The past is the past."

"For you, maybe, as you see only black and white."

"That's not true, but I don't embroil myself in the kinds of situations where revenge is necessary."

"Because you never had to defend your turf! This ogre literally wreaked havoc in my very home. He may not have been present physically, but he could have been for the devastation he brought."

"I understand, but he was right. He didn't make all the decisions."

The earl turned away, and she witnessed his anger return in full force. Perhaps it was of advantage to fight Swindon and find some kind of closure, but he might lose his life in the process. She stared hard at his set profile, her feelings stirring in her heart.

Perhaps he desired to die by a bullet or a sword. That could be his very wish. Or mayhap he would choose to live and sort out his problems, mend his life with Annie.

Elinor found she didn't know the answer. His actions were now like a rock rolling down a mountain with a life of its own. The rock would crush anyone who stood in its way.

With a sigh, she gathered the children. "I think it's time to go home. Cook will have supper ready for you."

The earl followed her without a word.

The next morning, Elinor rose with a heavy heart, but she didn't have much time to dwell on that, as Simon and his mother appeared at the mansion to see her. They knocked and stepped into the schoolroom just as the children were eating their porridge and milk.

"Elinor, my dear," Florence greeted her.

Elinor kissed the rouged cheeks. "You're out very early."

"We should've gone down to the country," Florence said peevishly. "There's no one left in town."

"Mother needs to gossip a great quantity of hours every day," Simon said good-humoredly. He lounged in one of the hard-backed chairs, looking much too big for its narrow frame.

"Fiddlesticks," Florence said. "But I have to say it gets awfully quiet around this time of year. If we'd been at Lyons Court, we might've been invited to some house parties."

"I'm sure of that, Mother, but we're here."

"Because I have my grandchildren," Florence said. "And no thanks to you, Simon."

"I suppose I'm the inveterate bachelor, but you have two of each through Constance, so don't give me any grief."

"And I can't budge them from London. I don't understand people sometimes. Why would you want to spend Christmas in the gray beast we call London? Nothing but grime and slosh and boredom."

"Connie likes gloom and grime, Mother. She has no interest in pure snow drifts or white powdered tree branches."

"Hmmph!" Florence played with Annie's beautiful curls as the girl finished her breakfast. "Oh, how long it is since Connie had curls like these. I used to brush them until they shone like spun gold."

"I'm grateful you concentrated on hers and not mine," Simon said, winking at Elinor.

Florence sat down on one of the chairs. "Elinor, have you gotten anywhere with Lucas as far as Christmas plans are concerned?"

Elinor shook her head. "No, not at all. He's adamant about not celebrating it, but I think if he were to be confronted with lots of people in the Christmas spirit, he might join in. He's seemed more approachable lately."

"That's because of you," Florence said shrewdly.

Or the ghosts, Elinor thought. "He was also against decorations at first, but we've already decked the rooms with holly and mistletoe."

Simon smiled. "Let's go find some mistletoe, Elinor."

"You're incorrigible, Simon."

"You have to be an opportunist to get anywhere."

"Does mist have toes?" Alex asked innocently, and everyone laughed.

"So what is your suggestion?" Florence asked. "I could demand of him to use the house, but I don't want him to resent me."

"I suggest you speak with Mrs. Braithewaite and make your plans clear. The earl won't even notice anything. He'll think the preparations are for us. He won't be happy about it, but will tolerate it for the children." Elinor wondered if she should tell them about Lord Swindon and the looming duel, but couldn't bring herself to speak about it.

Florence leafed through some of the children's books on the table, but she seemed oblivious to the text. "All I want is for Lucas to be happy again," she said.

"He likes to wallow," Simon said. "I have no pity for him any longer."

"Hush, Simon! Lucas's situation is a lot more difficult than you've ever had," Florence said.

"Yes, Mother," Simon replied with a look of long suffering.

Elinor decided to mention her worries about the duel. "We met Lord Swindon yesterday, which was . . . well, disturbing." She glanced at the children, knowing she couldn't go into any detail. "I'm concerned because I believe there will be consequences."

Simon narrowed his gaze, clearly understanding what she was talking about. "It's been brewing for a very long time, y'know."

"I see, but why go to extremes?"

"Gentlemen deal with problems differently than females," Simon said. He stood. "I'd better go find Lucas. He'll need me to assist."

He left the room before anyone could comment. Nerves fluttered in Elinor's stomach. Perhaps Simon could dissuade the earl.

Lucas breakfasted on ham, eggs, and kippers, washing it all down with coffee. He had slept terribly, wondering how to find peace again. His thoughts had hounded him ceaselessly, going over and over the events of yesterday.

Up till the moment Swindon appeared, Lucas had felt something akin to happiness inside. Something had lifted in his heart, leaving a lightness he hadn't felt for years and years.

He was vaguely aware of the mixed scents of his breakfast and he chewed automatically, his stomach balking at the nourishment, as it was tight with tension. He wished to retreat and think of the warm feelings Elinor kindled in him, but the meeting with Swindon overpowered all other concerns.

Simon startled him out of his fog. "Coz, I'm surprised to see you up this early and stuffing your craw."

Lucas didn't know whether to be annoyed or to laugh out loud. "I can't say I'm surprised to see *you* at any hour of night or day," he replied, putting down his fork. "What brings you out so early?"

"Mother wanted to get out of the house, and we came to call on Elinor and the children. I never reject a suggestion to see Elinor," he added.

Simon served himself from the sideboard—poached eggs and toast—and sat down. The butler poured fresh coffee and left the room. The two men faced each other.

"What exactly are you expecting from Elinor, Simon? Are you truly interested in her?"

Simon stirred his coffee agitatedly. "I am. I've spoken of it lightly because I know she has no romantic interest in me." He sighed. "She's the only woman I know who is sweet, beautiful, and level-headed. 'Tis a rare combination. She's rather wise, don't you think? You're fortunate to have her teaching Annie."

Lucas looked away, disturbed by Simon's frank confession. He noticed a fleeting pain in his cousin's eyes as Simon mentioned that Elinor would never be interested. "I know."

"At least I realize what kind of woman I want to marry," Simon continued.

Lucas nodded. Elinor was the total opposite of Phoebe. She was responsible, patient, and, above all, kind. Phoebe had thought of no one but herself.

"I . . ." Lucas started, searching for words that would be bland enough, "like Mrs. Browning."

"Possibly more?" Simon stared at him hard. "I know you. Since Elinor moved in, you've changed."

Lucas nodded. "I can't deny that, but I don't know where it's going, and if you're interested in her, I won't push my advances."

"If you don't, I will. But as I told you, she's not interested in me."

"I doubt she's interested in me, either," Lucas said.

"She mentioned you encountered your nemesis."

"Devil take it, I wish she hadn't spoken of that!" Lucas pushed back his chair and started pacing. "I didn't sleep a moment last night for the anger boiling in my gut. I can't tell you how much it bothered me to see his calculating gaze fastened on Annie, a snake looking at a baby rabbit."

"That would be reason enough to plant him a facer," Simon said. "Did you?"

"I was very close. I called him out. Will you stand up for me?"

"Naturally, Coz. We'll have to be careful, though. If the authorities get wind of it, you might find yourself fleeing to the Continent."

"They won't find out," Lucas said, anger burning hot in his veins. "I'm afraid I'll kill him."

"If you do, you will have to flee."

"I nicked him once, but that wasn't enough," Lucas growled.

"But your own life is at stake here. Mayhap he'll nick you this time—or more."

"I don't care."

"I understand. But what if he happens to kill you, Lucas? I, for one, would miss you terribly."

Lucas looked at his cousin as if seeing him for the first time. "You really would?"

"Naturally, Lucas. I remember you the way you used to be—before. You might not have had an easy life, but you were my friend, not just family. And you were optimistic and perhaps—young."

"Yes. I was young once—a long time ago. At least it feels that way."

"You *are* still that person, Lucas."

"Be that as it may, I have things to deal with that are a direct result of my poor choices."

"Well, yes . . . but your life is at stake here."

"Perhaps, but that's better than having no life."

"Lucas, your reasoning has flaws, but I understand your viewpoint. Where is the duel going to take place?"

"I am waiting to hear from his seconds. It could be as early as tomorrow morning at dawn."

Simon didn't reply.

"Will you be there?"

"Of course I will, Lucas. There's no question about it. Mayhap this matter will end once and for all."

"That's what I want. I don't need to be reminded of my past any longer."

"Does that mean you will accept Annie as your own?"

"Simon, I have accepted her by giving her my name. 'Tis more than you could ask of any man."

"Yes, but Annie is a person, even though she's a child."

Lucas hung his head, feeling the burden of his failure as a father. "I just couldn't . . ."

"Yes," Simon said. "I understand. I always have."

Lucas closed his eyes. "Thank you. I couldn't do this without you. The matter will come to a close once and for all."

Sixteen

Three days before Christmas, Annie took sick with a high fever and a sore throat. Elinor bathed her hot brow and red cheeks. Nanny hovered with towels and a fresh nightgown.

"Why do children always get poorly on the brink of Christmas?" Elinor said. "I remember several Christmas seasons when I had one ailment or another as a child."

"Aye, it's as if all the excitement gets too much. There has been a lot of bustling of people around here lately."

"You know, as all the staff knows, that we're having a large family party here at the mansion. The only one who doesn't know is the owner himself. We've been sworn to secrecy. I'm sure, however, he's starting to suspect something different is taking place, even if he has little interest in the running of the household."

"His lordship is a shrewd one, no doubt," Nanny said, handing Elinor the towel.

Annie tossed restlessly, her eyelashes fluttering in her uneasy sleep. Her beautiful curls were plastered to her forehead with perspiration. She tried to push off the covers, but Elinor held them down to keep her warm. "We'll have to stand vigil over her."

"I won't leave her side," Nanny said. "I feel sorry for her, poor little thing. She's so stoic and *alone*, even though she has us."

"I know she misses her real mother at times," Elinor said, looking at the girl's flushed face.

The nanny lowered her voice. "That woman wasn't much to miss. Nothing but tantrums and complaints. I don't think she even liked children, nor did she care for his lordship. 'Twas plain to see."

"Then why did she marry the earl?"

"Had to wed someone, didn't she? The earl was the best catch of his day, and she knew that."

"I could never marry on calculation alone," Elinor said, shaking her head.

"You're not anything like her, and I'm like you. I would only marry for love." Nanny's rosy lips turned down at the corners. "That is, if I could ever find someone."

Elinor smiled. "I've noticed that the second footman is particular in his attentions."

"James? He's a great big looby if ever there was one," Nanny said, but she looked pleased.

"A nice man nevertheless."

"Aw, don't say anything else." Nanny sat down next to Annie's cot, and Elinor rose.

"Christmas is around the corner, and we shall pray for health and happiness," Elinor said. "I'll relieve your vigil in a couple of hours."

She went downstairs, where the servants were in

the process of cleaning the chandelier crystals in the ballroom. Two footmen stood perched on top of ladders to reach the fixtures. They placed new candles in the holders, and maids were washing the windows while singing and whistling.

"This is wonderful," Elinor said and clapped her hands together in excitement.

She so enjoyed the spirited mood of the servants, so different from the usual gloom. Everyone wanted to be happy, she thought. Only the earl wallowed in the shadows.

Walking across the shining floor, she looked out the window at the dormant garden below. Flower urns carried high mounds of snow, and chickadees and sparrows foraged on the terrace where Cook evidently had thrown some old bread.

Elinor sighed and wished things would change with the earl. She remembered the compliments he'd given her in the carriage, and she longed to hear more. The realization bothered her. More than anything, she wanted to unite Annie with her father so that they could build a relationship, hopefully a positive one, Elinor prayed. It was a difficult position.

She watched the progress of the servants for a short time. She knew Florence had ordered flowers from hothouses to decorate the vases, and long tables had been put up for the coming feast. Florence didn't hold her purse strings too tight, if the preparations were an indication.

The kitchen space staggered under all the food that had been delivered in the last day or so.

She went out into the hallway and closed the door behind her. Wondering if it had been a good thing to keep the earl in the dark about the preparations, she walked to the stairs.

The library door opened and she heard male voices. Lucas and Simon came out, talking in earnest. She greeted them, knowing something had happened.

"Is something the matter?" she asked after greeting Simon.

The men exchanged cautious glances. Lucas looked at her as if evaluating her sincerity. "Well, something has happened," he said at last. "Since you know about the duel, you might as well find out that we're meeting tomorrow at dawn."

"Two days before Christmas?" she asked incredulously.

"What difference does it make?" Lucas commented, his voice impatient.

"It matters to me and to Annie. What am I to tell her if you're not here at Christmas because you're dead? Or if you're laid up with a bullet hole through your chest?"

He looked guilty for one fleeting second. "That doesn't change anything."

She turned to Simon, seriously annoyed by now. "And you—what are you doing about stopping this madness?"

Simon wore an expression of discomfort. "Elinor, you have to understand it's a matter of honor."

"Silly rules!" she cried. "There's no honor in injury and death."

The men formed an impenetrable wall against her.

"It's inevitable," Simon explained. "I will stand up for him." He patted Elinor's arm. "Don't worry, no harm will come to Lucas."

"You don't know that. For all I know, Swindon is an excellent shot. And what about Annie? If you're not there, who will take care of her? She won't have anyone to protect her from Swindon's malice."

Lucas had the decency to look uncomfortable, but the mulish set of his mouth spoke its own language.

"Florence would take care of her, I'm sure, and so would Simon here. Annie has doting relatives."

"At least they have the sense to accept her as one of the family," Elinor said scathingly.

Lucas looked away, his eyes stormy.

"No need to worry about tomorrow. Lucas will be successful," Simon said. "There's no doubt in my mind about the outcome."

Elinor knew she'd lost the argument. No matter what she said, they would still meet Swindon at dawn. Angry, she almost wished the earl would be injured because of his bullheadedness, but the compassionate side of her wanted nothing to happen. Annie would be devastated. She loved her father, even if he never returned her affection.

"Both of you are impossible," she said and turned on her heel to walk back upstairs. She could feel them stare after her.

She sat by Annie during the afternoon, brooding

over the earl's meeting with Swindon. She wished she could stop it somehow, but knew nothing could prevent the duel.

Annie's fever rose late in the afternoon and she started tossing and moaning. Nanny had sent for the doctor, and Elinor bathed the child's face with icy water.

"Papa . . . Papa," Annie cried weakly. "Papa!"

"He's not here, Annie."

Tears ran down Annie's cheeks, and Elinor wiped them off with her thumb. Placing a cold cloth on the girl's forehead, she called to Alex, who was playing in the next room.

He stared with concern at Annie. "Is she going to get well, Mama?"

Elinor nodded. "I'm sure. Alex, you can help."

He brightened. "How?"

"Go downstairs and ask the butler to take you to the earl. Ask him to come upstairs to Annie's room."

"Yes, Mama." Alex ran out of the room, eager to help.

Elinor hoped the earl couldn't deny Alex as he probably could her if she presented the request. She tensed as she waited. Would he care enough to appear? She decided if he didn't, she would never speak with him again, unless forced.

She waited and waited. Alex had not returned, and she wondered what had delayed him. She heard steps outside and her heart beat faster, but when she saw Nanny Wendell in the doorway, she felt bitter disappointment.

"The doctor is coming shortly," Nanny said.

Elinor nodded. "Did you see Alex downstairs? I sent him on an errand."

Nanny shook her head. "He was nowhere in sight." She went to change the water in Annie's bowl.

Elinor waited some more. When she heard steps outside in the corridor, she expected the doctor to enter, but to her surprise—and pleasure—the earl came in, Alex in tow.

"Your son is very persistent," he said, giving her a wry smile.

"He shouldn't have to be," she replied tartly. "But I'm glad he is."

"What is persistent, Mama?" Alex asked.

"It's a virtue, Alex," Elinor explained, knowing Alex didn't know what that word meant. She wanted to shame the earl, though he didn't look very repentant. He stood in the middle of the room, his commanding presence filling every corner, but she sensed his insecurity.

"Annie has been calling for you repeatedly."

He looked down at the sick child, and she started moaning, her transparent eyelids fluttering.

"Papa . . ." she called out, her voice raspy. Her little hands flailed, and Elinor caught one of them. Not knowing where she got the courage, she took one of the earl's hands and pulled him closer to the bed. Without saying a word, she placed his hand around Annie's and clamped it shut.

"You can sit here," she said firmly and rose from

the mattress. "There's a cold cloth you can bathe her face with."

Elinor decided to leave the earl alone to make his own decisions about how to act in the situation. She pulled Alex with her. She prayed the earl would connect with Annie like a real father.

She heard Annie's thin voice crying out, and the earl responded with some indecipherable murmur. At least he didn't ignore her. Drawing a sigh of relief, she went with Alex to the schoolroom and put him to work coloring pictures with one of the young maids.

She met the doctor downstairs, a pompous old man from Harley Street, and gave him an explanation of Annie's symptoms.

"Probably a simple fever, nothing more serious," he said.

They entered Annie's room, and Elinor found the earl stroking Annie's matted locks. He looked awkward, his large frame perched on the edge of the small bed. By the serious expression on his face, she sensed his concern.

"Dr Plankston, I leave her in your capable hands." The earl got up.

Elinor smiled at Lucas. "I'm grateful you cared enough to come," she whispered.

He didn't reply, clearly ill at ease.

The doctor leaned over the child and listened to her heart through an instrument that looked like a trumpet. The child started crying, opening her eyes and staring at her surroundings.

Elinor went to soothe her, holding her hand.

Annie noticed the earl. She reached out past the doctor and called out, "Papa."

He couldn't very well deny her. Clearing his throat, he took her other hand in his large one. "I'm here, Annie. Rest now so you can get well."

Pursing his thick lips and rubbing his chin, the doctor stared at the sick child. "She's caught a chill. Her breathing is labored, but not too congested. I'll give her some powders for the fever, and she should be better by morning."

"We'll keep a vigil all night, just in case," Elinor said.

"That is a sound decision," the doctor said and dug in his bag for the medicine.

Elinor met the earl's gaze across the bed, and she felt color heat her cheeks. A different kind of fever had come over her. Why did he have such power over her senses?

Annie looked from one to the other, then fell promptly asleep, her grip slackening. The earl tucked her hand under the cover and touched her downy cheek. He followed the doctor downstairs, and Elinor mixed the powder with water and awakened Annie. With Nanny's help, she made the girl drink and prayed it would work.

Nanny sat down by the bed and said she would take the first vigil. Elinor discovered how tired she was. Her limbs leaden, she went in search of Alex to make sure he had finished his supper. She'd forgotten to eat, but when she found that Alex had a plate full of bread and a crock of honey, she shared his bounty.

"Will Annie be well tomorrow, Mama?"

"I certainly hope so, Alex." She did from the bottom of her heart. She'd come to love the little girl as if she were her own.

Seventeen

Elinor sat at Annie's bedside at dawn. The girl's fever had not abated, but it wasn't worse, and Elinor had no fear Annie wouldn't recover. What worried her was that dawn was the hour when the duel would happen.

She hadn't slept at all, and a tight coil of tension prevented her from eating. If she didn't hear any news, she didn't know how she'd spend the rest of the day not knowing what had happened to Lucas. Stubborn men!

Annie was sleeping peacefully, so Elinor went to stand by the window, looking out over the snow-covered city. Smoke billowed from chimney pots, and people bundled in their thickest cloaks were walking dogs around the square. A weak sun was trying to come out, but the clouds lingered, dense and threatening.

She couldn't feel any kind of Christmas feeling. At this minute, she couldn't see any point in bringing all the festivities to the Lyons's mansion. Would the earl be bedridden for the celebrations, having acted willfully and selfishly by fighting a duel right before Christmas? It was the outside of enough.

He deserved to be run through for being so unable to put to rest his fury over the past transgressions of his wife and Lord Swindon. Wasn't it enough that Phoebe was dead? The object of his hatred had lost her life. There was no resentment to hold on to about that, but both of the men had chosen to be unforgiving and stubborn and full of righteousness.

"Oh, dear Lord, why does this have to happen now?"

She watched for the coach to return to Grosvenor Square as the sun brought full daylight to the world.

Waiting . . . waiting . . . waiting. She glanced at the watch pinned to her blue roundgown, and saw it was eight o'clock. It had been dark until around seven. The fight should be over by now.

She paced the room, every so often glancing at Annie. She touched her forehead, noting it didn't feel as hot any longer.

Would they be carrying the earl home lifeless in his carriage, or would he walk in under his own power? And Swindon—had he lost his life for having trifled with a married woman? Serious business, naturally, but was it necessary to lose his life over it?

Nanny entered, still in her nightgown and cap. She stretched and yawned, her eyes puffy with sleep. "How is she, Elinor?"

"Better, I believe. The fever has broken."

"I'm so relieved." Nanny bathed Annie's face and arms, and confirmed that the child seemed cooler and more peaceful. "I'm thanking God for making her well. Many children are swept away in this kind of fever."

Elinor nodded. "Yes, there's always that danger."

"She'll want to eat something when she wakes up, perhaps some broth or gruel."

Elinor was comforted by having something to do. "I'll go downstairs and speak with Cook. I'm sure she has prepared some for the patient." She ran along the corridor and down the curving staircase. Stopping by the windows flanking the front doors, she stared outside. No sign of the earl's carriage. *Where are they?* she asked herself, her stomach in turmoil.

"Dear God, bring us all together in the celebration of Lord Jesus's birth. Christmas tomorrow should be a day of happiness, not worry, but the earl has set up a series of events that might cancel the festivities and bring on mourning."

Not expecting an answer, she hurried to the kitchen, where she found Cook had made fresh gruel and also had a cup of hot beef broth. That would give Annie strength.

She brought a tray upstairs to the sickroom. Setting it down by the bed, she again went to the window to see if anyone had arrived. Nothing. Tension kept mounting within her, and she wanted to cry.

Something terrible must've happened, she thought.

"Would you like some of this broth, Elinor? You look as if you could use it."

She shook her head. "No . . . I'm not hungry."

"But you must eat to keep up your resistance. We

don't want you to become prostrate with a fever as well."

Elinor smiled. "Thank you for your concern, but I have an excellent constitution." Silently she reminded herself that her nerves were all atangle, but that in itself would not bring on a fever.

"If she keeps improving this quickly, Annie will be well in time for Christmas, no doubt," Nanny said.

"Yes, and a blessing it is."

"The earl has begun to acknowledge her. The servants are that surprised," Nanny said.

"He's been allowing himself to feel more, both pain and pleasure, and he's beginning to deal with the problems."

"That's a blessing for the little girl. We never had any luck when we tried to talk to him, but since you arrived, things have changed."

"I cannot stand by and watch Annie miss her father. Her little heart has been broken one too many times." Elinor sat down on a wing chair and pulled her legs to her chest as if to protect herself from the more nagging worry in her stomach: Where was the earl?

Dawn had come cold and blustery, heavy snow clouds threatening above as Lucas, Simon, and Lord Sinclair, one of Lucas's cronies, went to meet Lord Swindon in a meadow in Southwark near the tanneries.

"It's a nasty day to strip down to your shirt and

fight in the snow—dashed slippery as well," Sinclair said to Lucas, his voice disapproving.

"We can't wait until summer," Lucas replied. "The matter has to be cleared up, and this opportunity presented itself."

"Swindon will stab you in the back," Sinclair continued. "It gives me an uneasy feeling."

"You fear you might have to fight as well?" Simon asked. "I for one do not shirk a rousing fight. Can be very invigorating."

"Simon, that's deuced nonsense, if you ask me," Sinclair said. "At this ungodly hour, I much rather prefer my warm bed and a willing woman."

"You have a point, old fellow," Simon said with a sigh. "The question is where to find a willing woman."

They sat in silence, each man lost in his own reverie. Lucas felt that, yes, it would be a great thing to pull a sleepy and warm woman close. He never really had. Phoebe had wanted her own bedroom from the start.

Strange how she could still rule his life from beyond the grave. Besides, he hadn't seen her much during their marriage. He might even lose his life over her—someone who hadn't cared, who didn't even exist anymore. Somehow the logic of that seemed flawed, but it was all about pride at this point.

He could almost hear Elinor say the word *pride* with great contempt, but she didn't know what it felt like to have his failures thrown right back into his face.

Failures, she would say, *why dwell on them?* They were in the past, and hopefully he'd learned his lesson. Well, yes, he'd learned it. He would never marry again!

"'Tis starting to snow," Simon said. "Will possibly ruin your aim."

"So we're using pistols for sure?" Lucas asked.

Simon patted a case in his lap. "Aye, all decided. Your Mantons are in perfect shape, cleaned and oiled."

"The villain has a deadly aim, and the hair trigger on the Manton will serve him well if he plans to cheat," Sinclair said gloomily.

"Let's talk about my excellence instead of bringing in this gloom and doom," Lucas said. "You have me already dead and on a stretcher, Sinclair."

"Devil take it, Lyons, I don't want anything to happen to you."

"Lucas will be victorious," Simon said. "You nick him in the arm or the leg, and that will be the end of it."

"We're aiming to kill," Lucas said, angry.

"And make Annie an orphan? I don't think so, Lucas. You can't do that to the little girl. I'll never speak to you again."

"Blast it, Simon."

"And give Swindon the satisfaction of knowing that someone of *his* blood is getting all the benefits of your vast fortune, living in luxury in your mansions, and possibly finding a space for himself?" Simon continued. "To get Swindon out of the picture you need to beget a son, not die."

Lucas had thought of that before, and it annoyed him. It was too late to worry about that now. "This whole business is a damned nuisance," he said.

"Look at it this way: you have Annie. He doesn't," Simon pointed out. "Annie is the blessing in this case."

"I have sadly failed to see that," Lucas said, upset with himself for being too closed and full of pride. "Still, Swindon has been, and will continue to be, a thorn in my side if I don't deal with him."

"There are many ways to skin a cat," Simon said cryptically.

"What do you mean?" Lucas asked.

"Sometimes we might not have to resort to weapons, even if I personally at times thrive on the excitement. In your case, however, you have people depending on you. You can't just go out and brandish your sword at every provocation."

"I *never* pull my sword. I rarely wear it," the earl said drily.

"But you can be hot tempered at times."

"I still don't brandish swords, Simon."

Lord Sinclair looked out the window as the coach bumped across the rutted road. "We're almost there. I don't see another carriage among the bushes."

"Perhaps they are riding?" Simon said.

"If they are, they must think there won't be any kind of bodily injury. A wounded man can't very well ride."

"I hired a surgeon just in case," Simon said. "He's not far behind us."

"We won't need his services," Lucas said with a flash of anger. "I'll fight Swindon for the past and for his insults to Mrs. Browning. No one will die today, but I swear he will disappear from London. As you said Simon, I believe there's another way to get rid of him for good."

"Have you been working on it, Lucas?"

"I've done some investigation into Swindon's affairs, and I hope to prove he embezzled his nephew's inheritance, claiming that previous bad investments had ruined the boy. 'Tis always been known Swindon has a penchant for gambling."

Sinclair stared, wide-eyed. "Yes. Do you think he gambled away his nephew's money?"

Lucas nodded. "He's the boy's guardian and had access to the funds."

"But why would the bank let him take it out without contacting the family?" Simon asked.

"He has full guardianship over the boy, who is without parents. Evidently, he's claimed enormous medical expenses. The boy is always seeing some physician or other for poor health. There's always a chance the boy is being persuaded he has illnesses he never had. Two doctors allied with me have examined him and found him healthy in general. Quacks have given him so much medication he's not altogether coherent, but that could be expected. Swindon evades trouble from that quarter through liberal measures of laudanum, no doubt."

"Swindon must be queer in his attic," Sinclair said. "Bold as brass."

"Thinking he could get away with it," Simon filled in.

Lucas nodded. "I'm going to play this wild card. My solicitor will deliver a letter this morning to Swindon with everything stated, threatening prosecution. I never planned to fight him until he insulted Mrs. Browning, but I'll have to fight him here. He'll miss, and I'll present him with an ultimatum—leave the country or suffer the consequences of the legal system."

"You could've confronted him earlier with this. Why go to these extremes?" Simon asked.

"The investigation was just completed, and after the comments he made about Annie and Mrs. Browning, I do want him to stare death in the eye. After all, I have the reputation for being a deadly shot. He deserves to die, but I have no desire to spend the rest of my life on the Continent for taking his life." He thought for a moment. "Furthermore, I believe his suffering will be greater if he roams Europe penniless. He'll be an outcast."

"You were waiting for the perfect moment to confront him, weren't you, Lucas?" Sinclair said.

"I'm not without conscience, fellows. I've been debating revenge, but also remembering Phoebe went into this liaison willingly. It wasn't wholly his fault."

"Coz, you've been admitting her guilt, then, not just thinking she was a victim, as you tried to convince yourself in the beginning."

"You're right, Simon."

Simon lit up. "By Jupiter, at last! I've been waiting for a long time for that."

"I suppose I'm the only one who has been unable to face the truth," Lucas said. "But something has been shaking up the very foundation of my existence." He thought of the ghosts and of Elinor, who had done so much to change his life. She had made him see, but also made him believe he had another chance at love.

The truth of that had become more beautiful ever since he first realized it when they'd talked long into the night in the kitchen.

"There they are," Sinclair called out, pointing at another coach pulled up under a huge oak tree. In the gloom of predawn, the three figures looked threatening in their black cloaks, but Lucas felt no fear. Swindon would never be a threat to Annie after today.

Swindon and his seconds looked as if they hadn't had much sleep during the night, Lucas thought. His arch enemy had dark circles under his eyes, and his expression was ugly as he laid eyes on Lucas.

Good, let him stew in his own ugliness. People like Swindon always believe they can take whatever they want, no matter who they trample in the process. This is a big moment, not like that other time when I challenged him and nicked him in the stomach. This is completion.

At the same time, I'm validating Annie's existence. She's mine, and no one will tell me differently.

He faced his nemesis squarely. "At least you didn't turn lily-livered at the last minute."

"Why should I, when I have nothing to lose?" Swindon asked. "People like me are charmed. You're the one who should quake in your shoes."

"When the sun has brought full daylight this morning, your life as you know it will be extinguished, whether I live or not."

"You're very sure of yourself, Lyons."

"There's nothing I've been more sure of in my life."

"Your intimidation tactics won't work with me. I have no fear of you and your threats."

"As I said, you'll discover the depth of my threats by the end of this day."

Silence hung so tense he thought one slight move would bring the argument to a head with fisticuffs before the duel actually took place.

"Shall we get started?" one of Swindon's seconds asked coldly. "I don't relish standing in this biting wind."

Lucas stared into his wintry eyes and read the dislike there. Swindon had spread poison around, of that there was no doubt.

The seconds began examining the Mantons in their case for any irregularities, but Lucas knew there were none. He always fought a clean fight. One of the few things he did treasure was his honor.

He took off his cloak and coat, shivering in the thin white shirt. The wind bore down from the north, relentless and without mercy. Swindon's lips looked cold and blue. Lucas's feet grew colder by the minute as his boots sank deeply into snow with every step.

The seconds discussed the rules, and confirmed that the combatants would take twelve steps and turn around. At the drop of a handkerchief, Swindon would fire first, as he had been the one to be challenged.

Lucas could feel his hands shaking with cold and nerves. He knew Swindon's must do the same. He could feel the man's back against his own for a moment as they started to count out the steps. One . . . two . . . *Dear Lord, I ask for Your protection, but whatever happens, I ask for forgiveness for my shortcomings as a husband and father. I ask for peace for all in my household, and if I have to meet You today, I stand before You in all humbleness.* And he meant every word. Five . . . six . . . seven . . . *Thank you for sending Elinor to open my eyes, and please protect her. She must be one of Your angels.* Ten . . . eleven . . . twelve.

Strangely enough, he noticed every single needle on the yew tree at the edge of the meadow. The dark green stood vivid against the brightening sky. As he turned to face his enemy, he also noted the eyes of the small birds. They looked infinitely intelligent and also full of pity—but could that be?

Swindon faced him, his arm straight and his eye cocked to the sight. Everything happened in a split second. A wave of hatred hit him before the skies tore apart with the blast of the Manton.

Eighteen

Elinor was still waiting, her nerves so raw anything would have set off a tirade of frustration. She waited and waited and waited, staring out the window in one of the upstairs bedrooms that had a good view of the square.

They finally got back. The daylight was two hours old, and she feared the worst.

The coach rolled to a stop in front of the mansion. She ran downstairs as she saw a stranger and Simon help the earl out of the carriage and up the steps. He'd been hurt, but he still walked.

She wanted to cry with relief, but fought to control her emotions. She couldn't very well bare her heart in front of these men, not when she hadn't bared it in front of Lucas.

He looked very pale, and she saw his arm in a sling under the cloak that had been thrown over his shoulders.

"Is it bad?" she asked Simon.

"No, but we never thought Swindon would deny the gentleman's code of behavior. He shot before the handkerchief was dropped."

"And Swindon?"

"Lucas missed on purpose, but believe me, Swindon will not bother us again, and it's all very legal."

Elinor felt a surge of relief and stared at Lucas. His eyes held a veil of pain, but he beckoned her with the unharmed arm and she stepped into his embrace. "You must have that wound cleaned," she said, pressing her face close to his shirtfront, which smelled of good soap and starch. *He* smelled wonderfully virile and attractive.

"My surgeon already cleaned it. Just a flesh wound."

He leaned on her shoulder as the other gentleman helped get the earl upstairs to his bedroom. Lucas's valet took charge at that point, and those who had seen the earl arrive stared in concern.

"Just a small accident, good people," Simon called out to the knot of servants. "Go back to work now."

Elinor wanted to stay with the earl, but couldn't very well go into his bedroom as his valet divested him of his clothes and put him to bed.

Simon pulled her into one of the parlors off the master suite. "I'll tell you what happened, Elinor, and I assure you Lucas will survive the scratch."

He pushed her down on a red-and-gold damask-covered sofa and stood over her. "Lucas missed on purpose because he had other plans for Swindon." Simon proceeded to tell Elinor of the secret investigation the earl had ordered into Swindon's dealings with his nephew.

Amazed, she said, "He never spoke of it, nor did he spew much venom over Lord Swindon."

"Lucas has a great deal of patience, and he's very thorough."

Elinor nodded. "I'm reeling from all this information." Thinking about what he'd said, she readjusted the frill at her neck. She had to occupy her hands somehow. Her nerves still hovered close to the surface.

"All good news, really, except for the fact he was injured at all. You'll see, everything will work out in wonderful ways." He gave her a wink, his eyes sparkling with good humor. "I'm sure of it."

Elinor couldn't feel quite as optimistic. "I hope you're right, Simon."

That night everyone in the mansion knew the earl had caught a fever. Whether he had the same type as Annie had suffered, or if the wound was turning gangrenous, no one knew for sure.

Elinor didn't sleep at all. She made sure the children were cared for, but couldn't concentrate on teaching them anything. Annie had recovered quickly, but still showed signs of tiredness. She slept all through the morning when the earl went to bed with his fever.

Elinor could not help but worry, and when the doctor came out with the valet from the sickroom, he wore a serious expression. He saw Elinor at the landing by the stairs where she'd been waiting for him. She held her breath.

"There you are, my dear. I suggest that you help this good man in his nursing duties. He can't soldier on by himself, and seeing as you're a capable nurse, the earl needs you."

Elinor felt relieved that the doctor had commanded her to assist. At least she didn't have to wait endless hours for news. "How serious is it?"

"'Tis early yet. The wound looks healthy enough, and 'tis unlikely he would catch a fever from that so fast, but anything is possible. I suspect he's caught the fever that plagues London about now. Has the little girl recovered?"

"Yes, she's doing well," Elinor said.

"Just make sure his lordship is kept cool and that the light doesn't bother him." He slapped the valet on the shoulder. "Mr. Morris, don't look so worried. His lordship generally enjoys robust health."

"That's true," Morris said, his expression remaining the same.

The doctor left and Elinor turned to Morris. "Why don't you have Cook serve you a good meal and some strong coffee? I'll keep vigil over his lordship."

And she did. She sat at his bedside, bathing his brow just as she'd bathed Annie's. His cheeks were red and looked hollower than usual. She had never noticed how long his eyelashes were, or how bold and curved his lips. Her heart constricted as she remembered their kisses, and she could never again look at him without her heart making somersaults.

She worried endlessly about the fact that she'd fallen in love with him.

* * *

The earl floated on a strange cloud, then found himself in his bedchamber, a stark and barren room that had turned icy cold. On his bed sat an angel he seemed to know, but she faded into the wall, and another shape appeared, straight through the wood. He stood seven feet tall, sumptuously dressed in a fur-lined mantle that sparkled as if covered with stars. His white beard curled luxuriously around his smooth face, and his blue eyes twinkled with mirth.

"What's there to smile about?" Lucas mumbled.

"You—that you're stretched out here, helpless and humble."

"I don't see mirth in that."

"Touch my robe and I'll show you something."

"Who are you?"

"The Ghost of Christmas Present."

Lucas didn't even have time to touch the robe before they flew out of the house into the moonlit night. The air felt crisp and cold, but it didn't affect him, only invigorated him. Just as in the past encounters with a ghost, he could see the entire city below him. This time they stayed within London. The ghost pulled him through dark streets and the warrens of poverty at St. Giles and Whitechapel.

They stopped at a hovel where a meager fire burned in the grate, and people bent over small bowls from which came a sour smell. They looked gaunt and unhappy.

"You refused these people as much as a groat when they begged in the street. A small donation from your vast resources would've fed these people for weeks."

Before the earl could respond, the ghost whipped up a wind that carried them to another part of town, this one more substantial, but still modest. The ghost pointed a glowing finger through the window. "Look."

Lucas saw a group of people painstakingly counting coins and dividing them into piles. They looked kind and dedicated. Some warmed their red hands in front of the fire, and others peeled off layers of coats as if they'd been in the cold all day.

"They were outside from sunrise to sunset collecting funds for the starving. That's their focus this Christmas, to help others less fortunate."

"I have helped those less fortunate," Lucas said and explained about Cook's cousin and his poor relations.

"That was not your idea, though. You've lived a cold and miserly life, Lord Lyons."

"I had Brinkley donate funds to a charity I'd refused before."

"Because of guilt, not from the true spirit of giving."

Lucas pondered the ghost's words, knowing that mostly they were true. He would occasionally give to the beggars, but only if they persisted.

The ghost took him to the horrible dwellings of those souls, and the earl saw what good his money had produced. Their bellies had been filled, and so had their children's. Some new shoes to ward off the cold had manifested for the little ones, and a new wooden leg for the one-legged beggar had been purchased.

"You see what you're capable of, Lucas? And much more."

Lucas could see the difference even a small donation made to the welfare of others. "I've been closed into my own world for too long," he said.

The ghost showed him scenes from his life at the mansion and at Lyons Court, cold miserable days of loneliness. All the elegance around him held no significance when there was winter in his heart. In a sense, the stately refinement had less to offer than the hovel where love lived in the inhabitants' hearts.

"My life has been a valley of misery, but I'm beginning to see the true values," Lucas said.

The ghost smiled with delight. "I'm pleased, but you could still fall down into that dark pit if you're not careful." He pulled Lucas with a ghostly hand. "Come, there's more to see."

They traveled again through London, and Lucas recognized London Bridge and The Tower below. They floated down to street level at Haymarket, and Lucas recognized the street on which his secretary lived.

"Why are we here?"

"You shall see, and pay careful attention."

They stood by the window to the narrow house where Ian Brinkley and his family lived. Inside, the happy tumult of the children filled the room. Lucas couldn't count them all.

The giant ghost heartily sprinkled blessings from his hand on the door jamb. To Lucas it looked like gold dust.

"What are you doing, Ghost?"

"Giving something of my own to ease their way." He pointed within. "Look at their clothes."

Lucas noted the holes and the threadbare and frayed edges. "He shouldn't have so many children," he commented, knowing immediately it was the wrong thing to say.

"That is our Lord's judgment, not yours."

Lucas nodded. "You're right."

"There is Mrs. Brinkley. Have you ever met such a generous and friendly soul?"

"Perhaps not."

"Look at her gown. The fabric has been turned a number of times and mended, and the ribbons are of the cheapest kind. Would you want your wife to wear an old gown for Christmas?"

"No . . . but they have plenty to eat. I make allowance for extra food every week."

"I never said they were starving, and happiness is their constant companion. However, Mrs. Brinkley always has to turn the pennies to make ends meet, and Mr. Brinkley works until his hands and eyes ache abominably."

"He never complains. I'm not a despot," Lucas said defensively.

"And little Jimmy, his father's most treasured child. He needs an operation which might mend his leg, but where will they find the funds and the time? They slave from sunrise to dusk."

Jimmy looked happy but frail as he cheered on his brothers and sisters romping about. He'd never be able to romp, and Lucas noticed a pallor on his face. "He looks poorly."

Lucas experienced an unexpected pain in his heart, and struggled to catch his breath.

"That's it. The boy's heart is weak."

Lucas stared at the bleak possibility. "Will he die?"

The ghost showed him an inner picture where the whole family sat in mourning at the dinner table and Jimmy's place was empty.

"Oh, no, that will break Brinkley's heart. Is there something I can do to help?"

"I can't answer that. You have to search *your* heart for answers, and act accordingly."

Lucas felt a sense of loss for a moment, but there had to be something he could do. "I appreciate Ian Brinkley. He's been honest and loyal to a fault."

"Have you ever told him?" the ghost wanted to know. He glowed with a blue light that shimmered and sparkled, and Lucas thought he'd never seen something that heavenly and pure. The ghost's eyes glittered star-like, filled with compassion.

Lucas shook his head. "Come to think of it, I've never mentioned it to him."

"Without him, your life wouldn't run so smoothly."

"Yes . . . you're right, of course."

Lucas stared at the scene through the window and wondered if there was something he could do to change the future for Jimmy. He would do anything to help. Mrs. Brinkley finished laying the

Christmas table, and everyone's faces glowed with pleasure.

The family gathered around the dinner table and the children burst into a Christmas song as Mrs. Brinkley cut into the turkey and divided the food. To his relief, Lucas saw everyone had enough to eat.

After dinner and pudding had been served, Mr. Brinkley doled out a small measure of punch to everyone in the family. They cheered those not present and sent prayers to those who needed it.

"And a cheer to Lord Lyons," Mr. Brinkley called out at last. "Merry Christmas and a long life to him!"

"Oh, that miserable man. He doesn't believe in the Christmas spirit, nor does he share an ounce of your loyalty, Ian. I don't see how—"

"'Tis Christmas, my dear."

She reluctantly raised her glass and looked into his smiling face. "He thinks Christmas is humbug, and still you wish him good health and a long life."

"He's the one who puts food on our table, my dear."

"You're right, Ian. I wish him a merry Christmas and happy new year—wherever he is."

Lucas felt such unbearable guilt that tears pressed into his eyes, but also felt blessed to have Mr. Brinkley in his employ. After Christmas the Brinkleys would find their lives had changed for the better, and next Christmas they would raise their glasses in cheers without reservations.

Lucas turned toward the ghost and found that

the enormous and happy apparition had disappeared.

In his place stood a specter clothed in a voluminous black cloak, his face a darker hole than the fabric itself. Unseen eyes among the folds fixed upon Lucas intently.

Lucas shied away automatically, fear filling his heart. "Where did the Ghost of Christmas Present go?" he asked, knowing the question was useless even as he opened his mouth.

"He has left." The phantom stepped closer, his demeanor menacing. "I am the Ghost of Christmas Future, and I will show you where you'll find yourself if you don't change your ways."

Lucas bent down on one knee as if he'd lost the strength to remain upright. Dread filled every inch of his body.

The phantom pointed with a spectral hand toward a thick black mist.

Lucas's head spun crazily and a whirlwind took him up and out of Brinkley's neighborhood and out of London. He was aware of the soaring wind, but had no clue where they were going. Mayhap he had already died and this was his escort to the other side. *No, what is this?* He stared and stared as they lowered to the ground.

He immediately recognized the family graveyard at Lyons Court, the crosses and the stately obelisks raised by his ancestors. He stared at a marble angel holding a plaque as if it alone drew more interest than all of the others together. In gold, his name had been engraved in large letters, and he saw his birth date and the day of his death—Christmas Day, 1814? *That's the day after tomorrow! No,* he shouted, but not a word left his lips.

Snow lay heavy at the base, and a few dry leaves rattled in the tree above. Never had he seen a more dismal scene.

"You already have a life-threatening fever, and your life has been miserable and filled with self-pity. Perhaps it's time to focus on someone else's welfare besides your own," the phantom said. "It's not wrong to care for yourself, but sometimes you have to be pushed to serve others so you can better see reality."

Lucas saw that the specter spoke the truth. The bony skeleton fingers reached toward him. Power raised him again into the air and in his next breath, a deep and painful one, he found himself in his bed, burning up. Death was staring at him from the corner of the room, an insubstantial and dusty presence that exuded relentless power.

He heard the ghost's last words fading away: "It's your choice."

Nineteen

"Choices?" he said out loud, his mouth thick and dry.

"You're awake, then."

He heard a sweet female voice that sounded so familiar and close to his heart.

"Is he awake?" another voice, this one also female and familiar asked.

"He's muttering, but he hasn't opened his eyes," the first woman said.

Where had he met her before? He struggled to open his eyes, which felt gummy and burning to a point of pain. Why didn't he seem able to open his eyes? What was wrong with him?

Mayhap I'm already dead, and these women are my deceased dear ones. But his arm felt unaccountably heavy. What had the ghost or Death, that old friend-cum-enemy, said? *You're already dying.* He must be, then, because he couldn't feel much worse.

A cool hand touched his brow, and a wet cloth moved over his face. Ahhh, so soothing. Her fingers lay gentle on his skin, soft and caring.

The other woman, whom he suddenly recognized as Aunt Flo, said, "I think he's coming to."

"The ice water is helping."

"He's drenched through from all that perspiration. Morris and one of the footmen will have to change his shirt and the sheets."

"So hot, yet so cold," the other woman said, her voice so full of concern. He could listen to that voice forever. "He's shivering uncontrollably."

Lucas caught his teeth chattering, and knew he stood on the brink of the raging fire that would purify him, and the cold and eternal nothingness beyond. He tried to pull whatever was smothering his chest away, but nothing moved. His arms seemed to be without strength.

"Lucas?" the older woman said, and he managed to open his eyes.

Two faces hovered above him, one infinitely sweet, the other older and kind, familiar. "Where am I?" he croaked, every word an effort.

"You're in your bedroom, Lucas. I'm here with Elinor. You do recognize me, don't you?"

He nodded, and she smiled. Trying to lift his arm, he winced with pain. During an intense moment, he noticed the throbbing in his left arm, the pounding in his head and behind his eyes. Dear God, if this was dying, let it be over with soon.

"Your arm is wounded," Elinor said. "Do you remember?"

He turned his head to one side, but couldn't move it back as if to say no.

"And you have a fever, but the doctor says you'll live."

He closed his eyes to ponder his aunt's words. "Ghosts," he whispered.

"What did you say?"

The woman named Elinor repeated, "Ghosts. That's what he said. Perhaps he saw one."

"Fevers can play strange tricks on one's mind," Aunt Flo said. "Nothing is real."

As real as you are, he thought. An urgency filled him. If he wanted to live, he would have to mend his ways. He couldn't just lie here and wait for Death to catch up with him. He had to start anew.

"He struggles to get up," Aunt Flo said, her voice annoyed.

"Damnation," he muttered. "Let me go."

"The poor man is so ill he's delusional."

Hands pushed him down, and he wanted to scream with frustration, but darkness crept into his vision, and the pain slowly faded away. Peace came over him, and he decided there was no reason to hurry after all.

Elinor stared at his fevered face and kept bathing it. His beautiful black hair was damp and curled around his ears, making him look younger. Tenderness filled her heart and spilled over. Tears clouded her eyes, but she didn't want to cry in front of Florence.

"I'll sit with him for a while if you want to rest."

Elinor nodded and sought a wing chair by the

fire that had been built high. Totally exhausted, and feeling surrounded by warmth, she leaned her head back against the chair. Within minutes, she was asleep.

She dreamed Lucas kissed her, holding her so tight she thought he wouldn't let her go, not ever. His mouth moved sweet and warm against her own, and she sighed deep in her heart. A warm wind rippled around them and sunlight caressed them even as spring flowers sweetened the air. How he filled her with love, and how warmth filled every pore of her being.

She sighed, knowing he'd touched her heart like no one before, not even Matthew. Startled by that knowledge, she jerked awake.

"Is he still with us?" she asked Florence, her head spinning.

Florence smiled and nodded. "Of course he is. A puny fever is not going to finish off Lucas. He's much too stubborn for that. Go back to sleep. You nodded off for only a few minutes."

Elinor leaned back in the chair. "I wouldn't want Annie to become fatherless."

Florence paused before answering. "'Tis more than that, isn't it, Elinor? *You* wouldn't want to lose him. I have sensed the growing love between you."

"Nothing has ever been mentioned between us."

"But the air is full of it," Florence said, laughing. "It would please me no end to see you happily married again, and to Lucas."

"Married? You are about in your head, Florence. Why would the earl want to marry someone like me when he can find a duchess?" She held up her hand as the older woman opened her mouth to speak. "Florence, he's not one to marry just for love. He has to think about his lineage."

"Be that as it may, what happened with Phoebe opened his eyes to a different kind of union, one based on truth, compassion, and courage—not to mention love."

"Honesty is certainly something I haven't shirked. He's been the recipient of my sharp tongue on many occasions."

"He needed it to shake him out of his doldrums. You have done him a great service."

Elinor didn't know what to think or say about it. "I can only be myself."

Florence continued to bathe Lucas's face. He tossed and turned, moaning as he hit the wound against the mattress. "I don't know about you, Elinor, but I need a cup of tea. We both need strengthening."

"I can send down for it."

"When Morris comes back, we'll go downstairs for a good chat and a nice pot of tea."

Elinor nodded. "Yes . . ."

"I understand you don't want to leave him, but he'll be fine without you for an hour or two."

Her limbs heavy with weariness, Elinor leaned back against the chair. In a few minutes she began drifting off again. When she awakened, darkness had fallen outside, and she was alone.

She looked at the watch pinned to her dress and saw it was a little after four o'clock. Florence must've gone in search of that tea, she thought. Morris had not returned, but Lucas seemed to be sleeping peacefully.

She stretched her stiff back and rolled her neck. Still tired, but immensely refreshed, she went across to the massive carved bed. She shouldn't be here alone, but she was too concerned about Lucas to worry about her reputation.

Perspiration pearled on Lucas's forehead, and even as he slept, she sensed the struggle of his body. She found the bowl of cold water and started wiping the sweat off gently. Full of questions about her dream and about the reality between them, she sighed. Sitting down on the edge of the mattress, she prayed he would not be taken before she had the chance to find out the truth.

He had hugged her in reassurance when he'd returned from the duel, but mayhap she shouldn't read too much into it.

Half an hour later, he awakened, his eyes filled with the fire of fever, but he looked at her, completely aware of her presence. He gripped her hand as it lifted with a fresh cold cloth. She met his gaze as he released the cloth and clutched her fingers. Pulling them to his lips, he gave her a butterfly kiss. "Elinor."

She nodded, trembling as she tried to think of something to say, but she couldn't find the words.

"You are my guardian angel," he added, his voice thick.

"No . . ." She laughed with embarrassment and

tried to pull her hand away, but he held on to it. His skin burned against hers. "You're so hot."

"I'm in agony," he said, "but I don't care."

"Simon told me what happened, and what you found out about Lord Swindon."

"He won't plague London again."

"Annie is safe."

He sighed, his gaze floating away from hers for the first time since he woke up. "How is she?"

"She has recovered, and we expect you to recover before Christmas Eve tomorrow."

"That's a tall order. My arm is aching like the devil."

"That's for all the anger you carried for Swindon since you found out the truth," she said.

He sighed. "Yes. My hatred is diminishing. I cannot move forward and still dwell on past injustices."

She nodded. "You've changed so much."

"It frightens me. I don't know who I am anymore." He put down her hand at last and wiped his forehead on his shirtsleeve.

"'Tis nothing to be afraid of, Lucas. Life can only get better."

His face took on a haunted look, and his eyes still burned with an inner fire. "I had two other visitations, this time from the Ghosts of Christmas Present and Future. The first loomed enormous and had quite a jolly character."

She listened in amazement as he retold all the details of the ghosts, including the dark message of the Ghost of Christmas Future. "No wonder you're afraid," she said.

"Do you think it was real or the ravings of my fevered mind?" He sounded insecure and full of doubt.

"You believed in the others, and this really is a continuation of the story of your life—"

"And what will happen if I don't change."

"Yes, but don't you see? You've changed already."

"There's so much more to accomplish, Elinor."

"First you have to get well."

He smiled. "Nothing can stop me."

She wished he would talk about his feelings, but he didn't speak and didn't touch her again. After some time he tired and fell back asleep.

Half an hour later, Florence returned, leading Annie by the hand. "She kept asking for her father, so I decided to let her make a visit. Is he asleep?"

"Yes, but barely."

Annie clambered up on the bed, her legs tangling in her dress. She still looked tired, but had all the buoyancy of young children. "Papa?" she called out, waiting expectantly for him to speak with her, her legs curled under her.

His eyes flew open, and Annie patted his knee. "Papa, I'm here to make you well."

"Oh . . . you are?" For a moment he looked uncomfortable, but then he smiled. "That's good of you, Annie."

"I was sick too, Papa."

"I know. I worried about you, muffin."

Annie giggled at the unfamiliar endearment. "Papa, I want a kitten and a dog."

"There are many at Lyons Court. We're going

home soon, and you can have as many animals as you like—gray, white, orange, striped, or spotted."

Annie looked inordinately pleased. "Thank you, Papa. I'd like a white kitten."

"That should not be difficult. We'll find a mama cat with a young litter."

"A mama cat, just like Mrs. Browning," Annie said for no obvious reason.

Elinor wondered where she got the association, but Florence laughed.

"Yes, Annie, just like Mrs. Browning," Florence said, her voice bubbling with mirth. "And that makes *you* a kitten, Annie."

The girl giggled with delight. "I'll sit on your lap and have my chin tickled."

"But you don't purr," Florence pointed out, and Annie looked thoughtful. She jumped down from the bed and went to stand by Lucas's pillow. "Papa, would you like me to find a kitten that would purr for you and make you better?"

He turned his head and smiled. "You're all the kittens we need, and you've made me feel better."

Annie's face lit up. "Really?"

"Most definitely. I'll be well by tomorrow."

Annie danced around the room until Florence caught her. As they walked to the door, Florence addressed Elinor. "Tea is served downstairs, my dear. Morris will relieve you shortly."

"Thank you." Elinor felt torn between staying at Lucas's side and a heavenly cup of tea.

Obviously he read her hesitation. "You can't do

much more for me, Elinor. I'm feeling better, and you need some sustenance."

I'll miss you, she thought. "I worried a lot about you, Lucas."

"No need to, my sweet. I know I won't die. In fact, I've decided to be back on my feet by tomorrow, as I told Annie. 'Twould be excessively rude to stay abed on the eve of Christmas."

Elinor laughed. "That would be uncouth indeed."

"And I'm finished with feeling sorry for myself. The vicious circle has been broken at last. It's as if a big burden has been lifted from my shoulders. I'm starting a new life, Elinor."

She wondered if his plans included her at all, but he didn't mention her as he described some of the changes he envisioned. Even though she knew better than to pin her hopes on the impossible, her heart filled with sadness.

Twenty

The earl indeed improved rapidly. He slept four-teen hours and got up in good vigor the next morning, feeling at peace, as if he had indeed passed through the fires of purgatory.

The fever had left him somewhat weak, but he knew he would recover his full strength within days. Even the wound in his arm had stopped throbbing and, as Morris had rebandaged it, he'd commented on the quick healing taking place.

He dressed rapidly in a fine white shirt, pan-taloons, and a new coat Weston had designed and fashioned for him. His neckcloth obeyed his efforts and fell into perfect folds.

Today was a new day, a new life. Christmas Eve.

With a bounce in his step, he went downstairs. To his surprise, he found Brinkley in the library, bent over the clerical work that never ended.

"'Tis Christmas, Brinkley! What are you doing here when you can be at home with your family? Didn't I allow you the day off?"

Brinkley nodded humbly. "Yes, you did, my lord, but I have so much work to do."

Lucas sat down on the edge of the desk. "You're

always busy with my work, and I've never really noticed. I've taken you wholly for granted, Brinkley."

Brinkley smiled. "I don't expect attention, my lord."

"Perhaps not, but I'm feeling so joyful and optimistic this day that I want to do something special for you. You shall have a substantial raise that will give you more space for your family and better clothes on their backs, and I especially want to do something for little Jimmy. You shall take him to my doctor in Harley Street and have him examined."

Brinkley's face lit up with such joy that Lucas felt quite touched. "To find help for Jimmy will make me the happiest man in the world."

"You never complain or say a negative word about anything or anyone. This is a way I can show my appreciation."

Brinkley jumped up from his chair and clasped Lucas's hand with both his own. "Thank you, my lord! There aren't enough words to express my gratitude."

"Don't mention it, Brinkley. I'm honored to have your capable help." As he spoke the words, his heart seemed to soar with joy. Why had he always been so blind?

"Go home to your family. Enjoy a great Christmas feast." From his pocket, Lucas withdrew a roll of banknotes. He peeled off some and handed them to the secretary. "Buy only the finest from now on, my friend."

Brinkley bowed over and over, then threw his

cloak, scarf, and hat on and literally danced out of the room.

Lucas felt like dancing himself. He left the library and noticed the whole mansion smelled like cinnamon and fresh flowers. Flowers? He never ordered fresh flowers at this time of the year. Come to think of it, he *never* ordered flowers.

He stood irresolutely in the hallway and noted how polished and clean everything looked. The footmen walked back and forth carrying large bowls and trays filled with things that the earl couldn't make out.

"What is going on, James?" he asked the first servant who passed him.

"Arrangements, my lord." The footman walked on without any more explanations.

"What arrangements?" Lucas called after him.

"Christmas, my lord."

Lucas watched three footmen carry things upstairs. He deduced they were heading toward the ballroom, and he followed. In that large room, which had been shrouded in holland covers and dust since Phoebe died, servants milled around, executing Aunt Flo's bidding.

"I should've known you were behind this," he said to her. She looked festive in a burgundy empire-style gown and a tall turban decked with red ostrich feathers. Her diamond earrings glittered in competition with the pendant at her neck.

"And a most delightful time 'twill be, nevvy."

"I don't recall giving my permission for this." He watched as long tables were set with his finest linen and dishes. Candles sparkled everywhere, creating a festive mood. Crystal and silverware shone, and the chandeliers glinted with the reflection of so many lights.

"As my parents once owned this mansion and I spent many a happy time here, I took it upon myself to plan a Christmas gathering. Before the guests arrive, you can pour out all the gall and ire upon my head so we can get on with the festivities."

For a moment, anger overcame him at her audacity, but he pushed it aside. He placed his uninjured arm around her shoulders. "I thought of lambasting you, but you're right. You should be able to use the ballroom for your gatherings, and I'm sure I'll benefit from all the delicious food you have planned."

"Aye, you'll be pleasantly surprised, Lucas. In fact, I decided to do this not only for myself, but for you. It has been difficult to see your pain these last two years, and I wanted to help."

"You have been a great support, even if I've never told you. I was hiding in my fortress of pain and self-pity." He looked down into her eyes as she searched his. "Thank you, Aunt Flo. You and Simon have been my sanity."

"Not to mention Elinor. She, more than anyone, has helped you to move forward."

He looked down at the gleaming floor. "You're right."

"You ought to tell *her* that." Aunt Flo squeezed his arm. "Elinor is a most wonderful person, inside and out."

"Yes . . . I know." He sighed. "I'm afraid to open my heart."

"Don't you see, Lucas? You already have opened your heart. You're a changed man, and you have to tell her that."

"Elinor is a woman of strong opinions. She might laugh in my face, and I couldn't deal with that."

Aunt Flo slapped his wrist. "You big looby. Elinor has most tender feelings for you, and you would see that if only you had eyes in your head."

He pondered her words, wondering where his shyness was coming from. He'd never been shy in his life. "I'm as inexperienced as a greenhorn."

"That's perhaps the best way to be," Aunt Flo said with a tinkling laugh. "And Elinor can teach you a few things about being human."

"You're right—so very right, Auntie." He kissed her cheek. "When are the guests arriving, and how many?"

"Twenty, and I expect you to be ready and the graceful host at seven o'clock. We'll start with the Christmas wassail. That should thaw any frozen limbs and dispositions."

He laughed. "Your expressions are a tad cynical, don't you think?"

"I can't help that I see the truth, and I'm well aware of human follies. Lots of experience in that quarter."

"Yes, I suppose you're right."

"Why don't you go find Elinor and tell her about the new man you've become?"

"She knows—but I haven't told her how I feel about her."

"Today is as good a day as any." She pushed at him joyously. "Shoo, nevvy. Get those big feet of yours moving in the right direction."

He laughed, his heart hammering with both fear and joy. Wondering how Elinor would take his profession of love, he ran upstairs to the schoolroom. To his great disappointment, she was not there. Neither were the children.

He found the nanny folding clean dresses for Annie. She curtsied to him. "My lord."

"Where are Mrs. Browning and the children?"

"They went out with Mr. Nelson to listen to the carolers in the street."

For a moment, jealousy flooded through him, but disappeared immediately. Simon would do nothing to try to entice Elinor. His cousin had always been honest and totally trustworthy. "Do you know where they went?"

"She didn't say, my lord, but the children were most excited, talking about rocking horses and carved animals. Possibly something they saw before and have never forgotten."

"I see. I think I know where to find them." Lucas sent for his outer garments and ordered the carriage. Evidently they had gone to the shops in Bond Street they'd visited before. He couldn't wait to join them.

But disappointment filled him when he realized they had already left. "Did they say where they were going?" he asked the proprietor, who stood in a pile of woodshavings by the counter.

The kindly man replied, "No, they didn't say, but the gentleman bought some trinkets for the children."

Lucas glanced at the rocking horse, which was still in the window. "I want to buy that for my daughter, and I believe you have a set of carved farm animals with a barn and other buildings."

The proprietor turned very animated and spent long minutes describing his work and displaying every detail of the farm.

"I'll take all of the additions to the tableau," Lucas said. "Please have everything sent over to Grosvenor Square this afternoon."

"Christmas morning will be very special for the little ones," the old man said, rubbing his hands with pleasure.

"I surely hope 'twill be."

Feeling almost giddy with the joy of providing for the children, Lucas left. He walked the length of the street, meeting only a few acquaintances along the way.

At one corner stood a group of people singing the old Christmas carols. He'd always enjoyed them, except for these last two years.

His heart skipped a beat as he recognized Elinor in the crowd of onlookers. She was smiling and pointing out something to the children. They clung to her hands, staring and listening in fascination.

Lucas's will wobbled. What if she wanted nothing to do with him? It was one thing to speak of the heart in the throes of a fever delirium, but quite another to approach her as his usual self.

She peered over her shoulder and saw him. For a second her gaze reminded him of that of a hunted doe, but her expression changed to cheer. "Lord Lyons, what a surprise," she greeted.

The children greeted him with enthusiasm, and Annie clung to his hand. He quite enjoyed her little hand in his.

"Lucas," Simon greeted.

"We went out to buy some gifts," Elinor explained.

She looked beautiful in the light of the torches that the carolers had stuck into the snow all around. The singing flowed through him, and he sought for something nice to say.

"You always think of others, Elinor," he said simply.

"Christmas is a time for giving." She pointed at a tin one of the carolers carried. "They are singing to help the poor."

Lucas remembered a scene that one of the ghosts had shown him, kindly people sitting around a table counting coins. He might have refused to give in the past, but this time he felt only pleasure when he reached into his pocket and pulled out his roll of banknotes. Without hesitation, he walked forward and pushed them all into the tin.

The smiles that thanked him and the song that poured pure and soaring around him made him want to jump up and kick his heels together. "I feel so good," he said to Elinor. "So happy."

"Must be a novel feeling," she said drily, but she smiled.

"I didn't hear that," he replied.

Simon slapped Lucas on the shoulder. "Old fellow," he said.

Lucas winced and closed his eyes as pain shot through his arm. "Damnation, Simon."

"Sorry, Lucas. I forgot. How is your badge of valor?"

"Middling, but I'll live." Lucas looked at the children. "Are you enjoying yourselves?"

"Yes!" they cried in unison, jumping up and down.

"I suppose you've found out about the festivities later tonight?" Simon asked.

"Your mother cannot be stopped when she gets an idea into her head," Lucas said, "but I'm actually looking forward to it. The mansion has been too quiet for too long."

"Mother will be happy to change that, I'm sure. She loves to plan balls and routs—not to mention weddings."

"She always was a busybody."

"That she is," Simon said with a laugh. "She does like to give advice, no matter the subject."

"Let's go find her," Elinor said. "I for one look forward to the dinner party."

Aunt Flo made sure the mansion sparkled and gleamed for the guests, who started arriving around seven. Winslow, the butler, wore his best dark suit and the footmen wore newly powdered wigs and laundered white stockings. Their uniforms glittered with gold braiding, and they wore their haughtiest expressions.

"*There* you are, young people," Aunt Flo said as the earl came downstairs, followed by Elinor a few moments later. "You look beautiful, Elinor."

Lucas looked at Annie's governess. Elinor wore a pearl gray silk gown with some gauzy white fabric floating over her arms and shoulders, which were otherwise almost bare. Her lovely pale skin invited his touch, and he longed to pull her close and smell her sweet scent. Her red hair had been curled and gathered into a cluster on top of her head and surrounded by a band of fabric that glittered and sparkled as she moved.

Pearls gleamed softly at her throat, and her begloved hand held a hand-painted fan of great delicacy.

"You look exquisite, Elinor," he whispered and kissed her hand.

"You look very elegant," she replied, her gaze caressing his black coat and the neckcloth folds that had taken half an hour to achieve. He wore his wounded arm in a black silk sling, which gave him a mysterious air.

"Go greet the guests, Lucas," Florence said. "They are arriving."

Lucas had difficulty tearing his gaze from Elinor, but he had to do his duty, which he hadn't done for so long. It felt so unfamiliar, but good to be back in his element. The guests were mostly elderly family members of the Nelsons and some of his parents' cronies. Constance and her children arrived. Three of Simon's friends came with Simon and were immediately interested in Elinor. Simon had wasted no time in joining her, Lucas thought.

He looked at them and knew he wanted to make her his own. Fear shot through him at the thought, but he couldn't bear losing her. Sighing, he sensed a movement in his heart, as if it were opening and spreading.

The guests chatted and laughed around him, all in their best clothes and jewelry. Footmen offered sherry and champagne, and he accepted a glass without noticing what he was drinking until the bubbles tickled his nose. This is what it would feel like to bury his nose in Elinor's hair, tickling irresistibly.

"Merry Christmas, Lucas," one of Aunt Flo's female friends saluted him.

"Merry Christmas, Lady Agatha."

The dinner consisted of clear beef broth, white fish in aspic, geese, game, oysters, turkey, and every kind of vegetable available in the middle of winter. Aunt Flo had outdone herself, all the way down to the pink ices, creams, and the spiced and sugared cakes. The dinner party was a rousing success, Lucas thought.

After dinner, fatigue overcame him. He still hadn't gathered all of his strength. So much had happened in the last few days, and he hadn't had a chance to really think about it. Still, he didn't have a lot of time to think now. He had to act.

How would he approach Elinor with the burning question on his mind?

Twenty-one

Elinor knew something important was going through Lucas's mind. Every fiber of her being sensed his attention on her all evening, even if she didn't have a chance to speak with him in private. His gaze fixed on her every few minutes, making it difficult for her to concentrate.

She had difficulty breathing, and she wondered if he suffered the same. Simon paid her attention, but he also had his eye on the daughter of one of his mother's friends.

At the end of the evening, she was tired. Lucas looked fatigued as well, his skin pale, dark smudges under his eyes. He stayed to take farewell of the guests.

She went to see if the children slept peacefully and found Cook had sent up ices and cakes. Elinor hoped they wouldn't wake up with a belly ache.

When she returned downstairs, Lucas had retired. Aunt Flo still fluttered around, very happy with the evening.

"Thank you, Florence. I enjoyed myself royally."

"So did I!" Aunt Flo clapped her hands together. "What a smashing success. If this had happened during the Season, I would have been the talk of the town."

"I'm certain of it. You'll stay with us, won't you?"

"I'm not going outside in this weather." She pointed toward the window. "It's snowing heavily again. We'll be snowed in if it continues in this vein."

"We have nowhere to go, so I don't mind."

"You always have a good reply to everything, Elinor. 'Tis most annoying."

Elinor laughed. "I don't know if I can sleep after all this excitement."

"I won't have a problem after all the champagne I consumed," Aunt Flo said with a giggle. "Oh, my, I'm quite dizzy."

Arm in arm, they went upstairs together. Elinor knew she would have to wait until the next day to find out what was going on in Lucas's mind. That is, if he decided to share it with her.

When all was said and done, she didn't sleep a wink all night. Silence enclosed her, inside and out. She stared out the window and found that the snow lay deep. It had stopped snowing, and pale moonlight reflected off the pristine drifts. Blue shadows contrasted with the white, and nothing moved. People were hiding in their houses on a bitter night like this, mayhap sleepless like herself.

She couldn't get Lucas off her mind.

* * *

He dreamed about Elinor, his dreams full of wonder—but also worry she would fade away before he had a chance to make her his own. His arm ached. When he woke up, darkness still held the world in its grip. He lay in the night trying to recapture the sleep that had claimed him as soon as he'd put his head on the pillow, but it wouldn't come.

Morning couldn't come fast enough.

He lay sleepless until the first rays of dawn infiltrated the blackness outside. Groaning, he got out of bed, still feeling somewhat off after the fever. Today might be the most important day of his life.

He remembered the ghosts and how they had made him see the truth, and he was grateful, even if he'd been frightened as they appeared. He couldn't have gone on much longer with his old way of life. Bitterness would've killed him.

At sometime since the first ghost appeared, he'd found he could forgive Phoebe, and Annie certainly wasn't to blame for what had happened—or not happened—between him and Phoebe.

Waking Morris, who slept in a small adjoining chamber, he ordered a bath and the finest coat he owned. He luxuriated in the bath for almost an hour. Then Morris shaved him and helped him on with shirt and neckcloth. The folds didn't lie to perfection, but they would have to do. He made sure Morris combed his hair with precision and brushed off his coat.

He wanted to be as near as perfect as he could when he approached Elinor.

The children's laughter met him as he left his room around eight o'clock. At first he thought they were on the upstairs landing, but he saw them in the foyer downstairs helping Elinor light candles in the candelabra.

His heart began to thud hard as he saw Elinor looking beautiful in a white gown covered with a mint green spencer to close out the cold. Her glossy hair had been curled softly around her face and gathered into a chignon. To his eyes, she couldn't have looked more glorious than when she turned her gaze upon him and smiled.

"Good morning, Lucas," she greeted.

Her voice sounded sweet to his ears. "Good morning." He also greeted the children. Annie ran to him and hugged his leg.

"Papa, I have a present for you."

Touched, he patted her soft curls. "You do?"

"Yes, come quickly." She pulled him by the hand and Alex followed, clearly full of excitement. Elinor tagged along at the back. Annie dragged him to the kitchen, and there, in a wooden box on a blanket, slept a black-and-white puppy of unknown breed. "'Tis Rufus, Papa. We found him in the street, hungry and wet, and we thought you'd like him." She looked up at him with trusting eyes. "Do you?"

He bent over the sleeping puppy and patted its silky coat. "Of course I do. Among my dogs, he'll be my special friend, the one I take to town with me."

Annie jumped up and down and squealed. The puppy awakened, placed his friendly brown gaze on

Lucas, and wagged a stubby tail. He licked Lucas's hand.

"He likes you, Papa."

Lucas laughed. "The little tyke does. I like him, too."

Alex and Annie pushed each other and giggled. "I knew he would like him," Alex said with utmost pride.

Lucas rose. "I have something for you two."

Their eyes grew huge.

"Come with me to the library."

They all tromped through the house once more. Elinor had a curious look on her face, and Lucas knew he'd taken her by surprise.

"There," he said and pointed toward two cloth-covered shapes on the Oriental rug in front of his desk. "The tall one is for you, Annie."

The children immediately tore off the cloths, revealing the rocking horse and the farm with its carved animals. They screamed with pleasure, and Elinor took Lucas's hand.

"Thank you," she whispered, her eyes shining.

"It gladdens me no end to see the pleasure on their faces," he replied.

As the children played, he pulled her toward the window, where sunlight slanted through the ice-rimmed panes.

His heart pounded so hard he could barely speak. "This is a new day, a bright, shiny new day, and I wanted it to be perfect. So far, so good." He glanced at the children and smiled. "I want to see them grow up, both of them, under your wing—

and mine." He trembled as he lifted her smaller hand into his. "Elinor, you helped me immensely to change. You don't know how much you've helped me, and for that I thank you, but more than that, you've opened my heart."

Her eyes widened, and he could read hope in the blue depths. The expression gave him confidence. "What are you trying to say, Lucas?"

"'Tis difficult, but I'll have to be bold. I love you, Elinor, and I'm asking you to be my wife. With the children we'll create a family, and perhaps there will be many more—if you want to. I do, very much." Worried, he squeezed her hand, and she winced.

He apologized profusely, and it surprised him when she pulled him across the room to the open door. There hung a cluster of mistletoe from the lintel. She looked up at it and smiled mischievously.

"Kiss me. Then I'll give you my answer."

He pulled her into his arms—or arm, rather—and kissed her until dizziness overcame him. She responded with a passion he'd never dreamed of, and he knew the answer as he lifted his head to peer into her eyes.

"Yes, Lucas . . . I accept your proposal. Thank you very much."

"Are you as happy as I am?"

"Yes, I am."

He knew it was true, and she knew it was true.

"I love you, Lucas, more than I've ever loved anyone in my whole life."

"And I love you from the bottom of my heart."

They clung to each other, and when Aunt Flo arrived she cried out, "Well, well! This promises to turn out to be the best Christmas ever. Happy Christmas to you two, and I see congratulations are in order."

"'Tis the best Christmas ever," Elinor said dreamily when she could pull her attention from Lucas.

And it was, full of promise and laughter and love and merrymaking.

More Zebra Regency Romances